WHISPERS
of
TOMORROW

When love transcends the boundaries of time

A timeless love story by

KRITIKA MITTAL

INDIA • SINGAPORE • MALAYSIA

ISBN
Paperback 979-8-89673-815-2
Hardcase 979-8-89724-277-1

Acknowledgements

This book was born from a love so deep that I had no choice but to put it into words and share it with the world. It's the kind of love that's way too big for just one chapter (and possibly too big for my Word document to handle). So, here's to the kind of love that inspires you to write a whole book, and to the incredible husband who truly deserves a medal—probably one of those shiny, "Best Husband Ever" ones. Thank you for keeping our son happily entertained while I was lost in my own little world of words, constantly shifting drafts, obsessing over cover designs, and reading the same chapter for the fiftieth time. Honestly, you deserve more than just a thank you for that—you deserve a full-on parade. (Okay, maybe a fancy dinner and a foot rub. Let's not get carried away.)

Bangalore, 2021

A Conch Full of Memories

Being a woman is simple! You are only expected to think like a computer, work like a donkey, act like a lady, and most importantly, keep up appearances like a celebrity. Don't you think it sounds simple enough? In my constant endeavor to love, forgive, fight against stereotypes, advance both personally and professionally, and above all, always wear a sweet smile on my face no matter what life throws at me, I sometimes feel that I have lost myself! I've gotten lost in this whirlwind and maze of illusion called life!!

Like every other working woman, I'm no exception when it comes to juggling home and work. On the one hand, my son just turned four years old, and tackling his incessant questions and naughtiness is a humungous task that I thoroughly enjoy, and Arjun, my husband, is just an overgrown kid who needs lots of love and attention! On the other end of the spectrum, I'm a Program Manager working in an MNC. Balancing is the trick of the trade. Those who have mastered the art of balancing have attained what is known as "Modern Nirvana!"

As the launch of the product that my team has been working on for more than a year approaches, things have become hectic. Over the past few months, the team has been working with all its zeal, passion, and good spirits. Being able to work with people who mirror your enthusiasm and are aligned with your values is certainly a blessing. With all the hard work, sweat, and tears shed, the moment of truth has finally arrived! I was working from home on the release date as I had too many calls to take. I worked tirelessly throughout the day, patiently answering calls, attending heated discussions and meetings, and trying to smooth out the smallest of creases so that we could sail unhindered to success. When the product launch was finally deemed "Successful," I reclined, shut my laptop, dropped my glasses on the table, and glanced at the wall clock with flushed cheeks, reddened eyes, and drooping eyelids. It was way past midnight. My husband had taken our son to my parent's place, which was located nearby. He did it because he knew that I needed undivided attention to my work. As a result, there was no one else in the house except me. The room was filled with the warm, gentle light of a desk lamp, creating elongated shadows across the walls. I got up from my chair to get a glass of water and something on the mantelpiece caught my eye. It was a small conch that I found on the beach of Chennai. Smiling to myself, I picked up the conch from the mantelpiece and looked at it with subliminal eyes. There were so many emotions attached to this simple yet so beautiful conch. I remember it was during my first on-site assignment in India. My first corporate experience - away from home, alone in a different city with a very different culture and tradition. During my stay of two months in Chennai, a lot happened. More than just work and the workplace, I learned a lot about people and life in general. Those are still bitter-sweet memories. As I try to churn my memories of that time, the flashback lights up my face, and my hands tremble when I hear the phone ringing in the stillness of the night, with nothing but silence around me.

"*It was the best of times; it was the worst of times.*"

– Charles Dickens.

Chandigarh, 2010

Navigating the Unknowns

In a world adorned with a thousand sunny days, there was Kiara who seemed woven from the very fabric of joy. Her eyes, striking as peacock feathers, held a universe of dreams, sparkling with mischief and warmth. Her hair flowed like the spring breeze, cascading around her shoulders in a soft embrace, inviting all who crossed her path to linger a moment longer. She was a symphony of color, a rainbow of love that illuminated the hearts of those around her. Just as the endless blue ocean welcomes the shore, she enveloped every soul in her presence, offering comfort and connection. Coming from the vibrant city of Chandigarh, she had sharp features and deep-set eyes that sparkled with hope. She was a sight to behold, standing at a modest 5 feet 3 inches. Her long hair danced around her shoulders, framing a face that often wore a charming grin, concealing the complexities of her heart. Though her frail and lean body suggested fragility, within her burned a fierce spirit, unyielding and full of life. She can be delightfully known as "Aaffat," a title that reflected her goofy yet vibrant nature. Her laughter could fill a room, and her quirky sense of humor often lightened the heaviest of moments. But, beneath that playful exterior lay a tempest of emotions—sadness, rage, and frustration—that she skillfully veiled from the world. If only others could see beyond her smile, they would have been devastated by the broken pieces of her naked soul that she was attempting to mend on her own.

She loved adventures, her spirit a flame flickering with the promise of new experiences. She was always ready to embrace the rollercoaster of life, eager for every twist and turn it offered. To her, each day was a gift, a miracle not to be taken for granted. From an early age, she believed that life's beauty lays in its unpredictability, and she longed to explore the world and dive into the vibrant spectrum of human emotions. Since childhood, Kiara had worked tirelessly to push her boundaries, driven by a relentless desire to fulfill her dreams. Unlike others, she never fantasized about building palaces in the air but rather had concrete plans to build a life, a home. She was determined in her goals and unwavering in her beliefs. She was invincible when enraged. Her presence and aura in a roomful of people always set her apart. Whenever she speaks, her confidence flowed like a river, steady and compelling. Every word was infused with conviction, painting vivid images of her dreams and aspirations. Listeners couldn't help but lean in closer, captivated by her stories and the authenticity of her voice. "Big things often come in small packages." Isn't it? Possessing a lethal combination of sharp intellect and willingness to work hard, she was a rare unpolished diamond to whom everyone overlooked as a mere piece of broken stone. But who knew, everything was about to change!

Kiara was raised by her relatives, who treated her with persistent neglect from a young age. Her aunt, who was notably partial, ensured that her own children received the best of everything, often leaving her with little or nothing. While such indifference is not uncommon when caring for someone else's child, Kiara, too young to grasp these nuances, internalized the mistreatment as a personal failing. She felt guilty, believing that her aunt's harshness must have been due to some mistake she had made. With her attractive appearance, clear justifications, and charming voice, she tried to convince people that she was valuable. "Trust me, I can do it," pleaded the innocent face. Unfortunately, it not only fell on deaf ears but also deepened her despair. Her aunt's harsh words, "You will never succeed; you are useless," only compounded her distress. With teary eyes, she would recede to her bedroom to take solace in her bed and cover her face under her pillow, which became a silent repository for her anguish. Unable to share her feelings with anyone, she sought refuge in the pages of books, losing herself in their worlds to escape her own pain. Her face brightened at the sight of hardbound books in the library, her smile growing as she breathed in the mingling scents of new and old volumes. The library was her sanctuary throughout high school and college, and the staff, the librarians always greeted her warmly, recognizing her as a familiar face.

They would often chat over steaming cups of tea, unaware of her personal predicaments. Instead of seeking pity, Kiara was driven by a desire for admiration and a quest for knowledge. Her sheer enthusiasm for reading across various genres led the librarians to recommend intriguing titles, which expanded her literary horizons. Among them was Mrs. Singh, a kind and elderly woman who enjoyed Kiara's effervescent personality. Though she sensed that Kiara carried deep, unspoken pain, she never probed into her personal life, respecting her privacy, and valuing her presence in the library. They would spend hours discussing a wide range of authors, from Wordsworth to O'Henry to Kafka. Mrs. Singh, a well-read woman in her late 50s with over 30 years of experience as the college librarian, frequently suggested books from diverse genres. Through these recommendations, Mrs. Singh helped Kiara rediscover her inner strength, courage, and self-confidence. Often, Mrs. Singh would remind Kiara, "If you don't believe in yourself, no one else will," and this advice resonated deeply with her, becoming a guiding principle she held dear.

Kiara's journey was nothing short of epic. She had set out to conquer the world, her eyes locked onto the peak of her career like a hawk on its prey. The library, a place where the quiet hum of fluorescent lights was her only companion as she poured over textbooks and journals until her vision blurred and her head throbbed with the weight of knowledge. Each sleepless night was a testament to her resolve, her fingers dancing over keyboards and scribbling notes until dawn crept through the window like a reluctant spectator. The world, however, proved a cruel adversary. She faced a relentless barrage of setbacks—rejections, criticisms, and a sea of skepticism that seemed to rise higher with every stride she took. It wasn't anger that propelled her forward but a steady determination, a quiet fire that burned steadily within her. Her faith in her future remained unshaken as she believed that her perseverance would carve a path to a fulfilling career. Yet, destiny, it seemed, had a taste for irony. Though her grades were commendable and her efforts relentless, the job market was unforgiving. The job offers that once seemed like golden tickets disintegrated under the weight of an economic downturn, leaving her clutching at fragments of promises that never materialized.

With a heavy heart but a hopeful spirit, she ventured to Gurgaon, lured by its reputation as a city that presents you with boundless opportunities. But as the days wore on, the city revealed its own harsh truths. The skyscrapers that reached for the heavens were mirrored by the challenges that lay in wait for those who sought to climb. The streets of Gurgaon, bustling and bright, bore witness to her struggle, a stark contrast to the hopeful dreams she had harbored. Every step she took felt like a step further from the vision she had once held so dearly. In this sprawling urban labyrinth, she found herself grappling not just with the practicalities of job hunting but with the deeper question of her place in a world that seemed to shift beneath her feet. The challenges were formidable, but her spirit, though tested, remained undaunted. She had come to this city with a dream, and as she faced the trials ahead, she knew that the journey was far from over. Sitting on the edge of her bed and staring out at the sprawling cityscape of Gurgaon from her tiny apartment window, the skyline glittered with a promise of success, yet the view felt cruel. Her fingers traced the worn edges of her resume, now littered with notes and edits, the once-hopeful document now a testament to countless rejections. Each morning, she braved the bustling streets, her heart heavy with the weight of unfulfilled dreams. She navigated the labyrinthine avenues of the corporate world with a mixture of hope and trepidation, attending interviews that ended with polite smiles and the inevitable, "We'll be in touch." The days blurred into a haze of networking events, cold calls, and follow-up emails, each one another thread in the tapestry of her relentless pursuit. One particularly sweltering afternoon, she found herself seated in a sleek office lobby, the air conditioning a stark contrast to the heat outside. Clutching her resume tightly along with a bundle of her aspirations, she decided to return home after hearing the same, "we'll be in touch." Her days blurred together as she juggled the demands of a grueling night shift at a call center with the ceaseless quest for a career that felt increasingly elusive. Weeks turned into months, and the weight of her trials seemed almost too great to bear. But then, as if in response to her unyielding perseverance, the tide began to shift.

One crisp morning, as the first rays of sunlight filtered through her apartment window, her phone rang with an unfamiliar number. Her heart pounded as she answered, and the voice on the other end was one of welcome and an opportunity. The offer came from a renowned IT company, a beacon of hope in the sea of her struggles. The job was everything she had worked for, and more. The hours were reasonable, the salary respectable, and the company's reputation was impeccable. As she read through the offer letter, a sense of relief and triumph washed over her. The months of hardship had borne fruit, and she was finally stepping into the role she had always dreamed of. Her nights of toil at the call center were now a distant memory, a testament to her resilience and unwavering commitment. The dreary nights had transformed into bright mornings filled with possibilities. With this breakthrough in her career, her belief about the manifestations became firmer.

> **“** *When you want something, the whole universe conspires in helping you to achieve it.* **”**
>
> – *Paulo Coelho*

Gurgaon, 2011

The Dawn of Opportunity

Kiara was a bundle of excitement and anxiety as her joining date approached. Her mind, a commotion of questions and uncertainties. She was meticulous in her preparations, ensuring that everything was in place for her first day at work. Yet, this sense of apprehension was unusual for her - a stark contrast to her usual calm demeanour. Her wardrobe choices were limited, a testament to the modest budget she had been living on. As she sifted through her clothes, she couldn't help but feel a pang of frustration. Shopping was a luxury she rarely indulged in, not because she didn't enjoy it, but because her financial situation necessitated restraint.

"If I wear this, what will others think of me?" she pondered aloud, holding up a modest blouse and skirt. "What will people think if I wear such simple clothes in a place where everyone is impeccably dressed?" Her heart sank as she considered the polished, sophisticated attire of the MNC employees she had seen in the business magazines and during her interviews. Seeing this, her flatmate reassured her that it's your commitment and intelligence that will impress them, not your clothes. You aren't a runway model. Resolute, she chose the best outfit she had, ironed it with care, and managed a small, encouraging smile. She forced herself to relax and drift into sleep, her mind still buzzing with thoughts and worries. She knew that positivity and rest were essential, and she hoped that her dreams would calm the storm of anxiety swirling within her.

The next day, as she arrived at DLF Cybercity in Gurgaon, she experienced a sensory overload that left her breathless. The grandeur of the multi-lane roads, towering skyscrapers, and enormous glass atriums felt like a scene from a movie, a world that she had never experienced and was both exhilarating and overwhelming. The fifteen-story building where she would begin her new role stood like a beacon of opportunity, magnificent and imposing. The reception area was an elegant space, adorned with lush decor and a welcoming ambiance that seemed to hum with possibility. As she stepped inside, a stunning receptionist greeted her with a warm smile, instantly easing the weight of her apprehensions and inviting her to step into this new chapter of her life.

"Have you had breakfast? Do you want something to eat or drink, ma'am?" the receptionist asked.

Her polished tone catching Kiara off guard. "Who, me? Not at all. I'm okay," she stammered, surprised by the unexpected politeness.

The receptionist's courteous manner and the refined accents filled her with awe; everyone around her radiated an air of wealth and confidence. The perfectly polished boots, silk ties, and tailored jackets spoke of a world that felt utterly foreign to her. Just then, a soothing voice broke into her thoughts.

"Hello, I'm Nalini. Are you Kiara?"

Kiara nodded, her nerves easing slightly. "Yes."

"Please, come with me," Nalini said warmly, leading her towards the auditorium for the induction.

Kiara settled into an aisle seat, her heart racing as she absorbed the presentations. When the perks of the company were announced—highlighting a daily free lunch featuring a variety of cuisines—the crowd erupted in cheerful laughter, and she couldn't help but smile, her spirits lifting at the thought of such an unexpected treat. "Is this real? A free lunch every day?" she marvelled, impressed by the generosity. Despite a few technical hiccups with the laptop setup, she managed the induction with poise. Afterwards, Arjun, her hiring manager, arrived to escort her to her new workstation, a sense of excitement bubbling within her as this fresh chapter began to unfold.

As they walked through the office, she was captivated by its modern, open design. The expansive, airy space featured mobile desks arranged in a honeycomb pattern, creating a sense of collaboration and fluidity. Her new colleagues, dressed in vibrant, semi-formal attire, added to the lively atmosphere, complemented by an array of plants and striking artwork. A cozy coffee corner beckoned with its large flat-screen TV and plush sofas, while a snooker table provided a fun escape during breaks. "Have I arrived at an art studio?" Kiara wondered aloud; her eyes wide open with astonishment. The colourful glass walls of the meeting rooms and the overall aesthetic enveloped her in a sense of wonder, making her feel as if she had stepped into a different world. With a mix of excitement and trepidation, she absorbed her surroundings, realizing she was embarking on a new chapter filled with both challenges and opportunities. As she settled into her role, Kiara knew that although the environment was vastly different from what she was used to, her determination and passion would guide her through this exhilarating new beginning. Her expression of surprise caught Arjun's attention, and he grinned, the look reminiscent of his own first day at work. He introduced her to the entire team. As her teammates introduced themselves, wishing her success, she felt a swell of encouragement watching their camaraderie. Laughter filled the air as they playfully teased one another, creating an atmosphere that felt warm and inviting. After leading Kiara to her workstation, Arjun handed her a schedule for sessions that would begin the following day. Just as she was settling in, her new teammates invited her to join them for snacks. Initially hesitant, as she wasn't feeling particularly hungry, she was cut off by Arjun's cheerful declaration, "Now you are part of a group that eats together and stays together." Her childlike face lit up, a grin spreading from ear to ear, and her heart swelling with a sense of belonging as laughter and chatter enveloped her.

As the team's introductory courses began the next day, she quickly felt the weight of expectations. Each session brought increasing difficulty, and the dreaded "surprise" tests stirred memories of her school days, leaving her both anxious and nostalgic. It soon dawned on her that, aside from a handful of disciplines she truly enjoyed, most of her engineering coursework felt irrelevant to her new role. Frustration bubbled up as she wondered why they had been compelled to study six or seven subjects each semester when so much seemed unnecessary. Yet, amidst this turmoil, she began to adapt, learning to ride the waves of tests and the deluge of information. She realized that her biggest challenge in the office was not just learning but unlearning the excesses of her academic past. For a month, the twenty new hires endured rigorous classroom training, all striving to prove their worth for advancement. As a self-proclaimed lone wolf, she found it hard to connect with her more social peers and felt a pang of longing for the vibrant lifestyles they led. Still, she held onto a thread of optimism, envisioning a future where she could join them. Glancing at her meager bank balance, she reassured herself, "The necessity of the hour is steady employment for a sustainable cash flow." While memorizing countless passwords and mastering the intricacies of the products took time, her seniors noticed her swift progress after a few knowledge transfer sessions. Her intelligence, tenacity, and passion caught the attention of her superiors, earning her a spot as one of the company's "Early Talents." This recognition came with more than just accolades; it promised a mid-year wage adjustment, igniting a thrill within her. She was ecstatic beyond measure! She felt a surge of hope as she contemplated the possibilities that lay ahead, her heart swelling with anticipation for the future.

"You won't believe what happened today!" Kiara exclaimed, her voice brimming with excitement as she called her cousin Ananya to share the news of her wage revision. Ananya, always eager to lend an ear, replied with a chuckle, "Tell me everything! My lecture got postponed, so I have all the time in the world, sis." As Kiara launched into her story, her emotions flowed freely, unfiltered, and exuberant. She felt a comforting sense of openness with Ananya, knowing she could express herself without fear of judgment. "Guess what? My manager complimented me in front of everyone! And my pay is going up! I can finally go shopping and explore all the amazing food this city has to offer. I think I've truly fallen in love with this place! I'm just so overjoyed!" While she spoke at a rapid pace, Ananya listened with an amused smile, her eyes twinkling with mischief. "Sounds like someone has a crush," she teased, hinting at the details Kiara shared about Arjun. Kiara rolled her eyes but continued her enthusiastic recounting, brushing off Ananya's playful remarks. Their bond was unbreakable; despite the two-year age difference, they understood each other perfectly. Ananya, now serving as an intern at a government hospital in Chandigarh after completing her MBBS, provided a grounding presence in Kiara's life. The close aunt who had raised Kiara is Ananya's mother. As she spoke, she felt grateful for this connection, a steady anchor amidst the whirlwind of her new beginnings.

After being impressed by her performance and upbeat attitude, Arjun decided to assign Kiara to a project in Chennai, where she would execute a product for one of the company's largest clients in India. When he shared the news with her later that day, she felt a surge of excitement. This would be her first project involving direct interactions with clients and stakeholders, and, most intriguingly, she would have the opportunity to work on the system. Though she recognized the challenges ahead, she took a deep breath and responded with determination, "I'm ready for it."

As Joseph P. Kennedy has written "When the going gets tough, the tough get going."

From the outside, the business world often appears polished and perfect. But she had learned quickly—just two months into her career—that the reality is far more complex. She understood it to be a labyrinthine maze, one that required both cunningness and perseverance to navigate through layers of jargon, casual coffee corner conversations, and the inevitable office politics. In this bustling environment, finding someone to support you—someone who would genuinely say, "Hey, don't worry, I'm here for you"—was no small feat. In this concrete jungle, true friendships felt elusive, and meaningful connections, even more so. Yet, despite these challenges, she felt a flicker of hope. Perhaps this project would not only test her skills but also lead her to those rare colleagues who could become allies in her professional journey.

She often walked alone, a solitary figure navigating the complexities of her life. Despite facing challenging circumstances at a young age, she remained fundamentally the same kind-hearted soul she had always been. A wise individual once remarked, "You can repaint a house, but you can't change the foundation." Deep down, she was still that tender, naive child yearning for acceptance and love. When someone she trusted let her down, she would retreat into her shell like a turtle, quietly weeping into her pillow, never finding the strength to confront her pain. In her teenage years, the sting of sarcasm and rejection had cut deep, yet those experiences had also shaped her resilience. To protect herself, she built emotional walls, shielding her heart from further wounds. Still, beneath that facade lays an enduring desire for connection, a reminder of the warmth and vulnerability that defined her spirit.

"Visiting Chennai was thrilling, but how will I get there?", pondered her with a whirlwind of questions swirling in her mind. How did one purchase a plane ticket? Do I need to make hotel reservations? What about local transportation? Unfortunately, no one in her immediate circle was available to help. She had never bought a plane ticket before; she had never needed to. Summoning her courage, she used Arjun's card to book an early morning flight to Chennai. That evening, she left her workplace slightly earlier than usual, hurried home to pack her essentials, and rushed to the airport under the cover of night, thinking that it was the best approach. As she passed through the "domestic departure" gate, the security staff regarded her with a mix of curiosity and amusement. "First time flying?", she admitted with a sheepish nod. The security officer smiled requesting her ticket and ID. After passing through the gates, she approached another staff member. "Excuse me, sir, this is my first trip, and I'm not quite sure about the boarding procedures. Could you assist me?" With a blank stare, he replied, "Madam, it's all detailed in English. I'm sure you can read." Flushing with embarrassment, she turned on her heel and headed to the airline's assistance desk. There, a warm smile greeted her, and a kind woman patiently walked her through the necessary steps for check-in, security, and boarding. She sighed with relief. "You have no idea how much this means to me. Thank you!"

It took some time for her to navigate the check-in process, as the signage and multiple gates left her feeling bewildered. After clearing security, a wave of anxiety washed over her. Was it the intricacies of the project, the thought of staying alone in a hotel room, or the anticipation of her first flight to a different city that unsettled her? We constantly fear change, especially when we are required to make difficult choices. We are never certain how the shift will affect us—whether it will crash into our lives like a wave or advance gradually like a melting glacier. The only choice we have is to embrace it. Kiara embraces the journey ahead, relinquishing her tightly held plans and accepting whatever awaited her. Life, with all its unpredictability and challenges, was a canvas yet to be painted, and she was ready to see what colors the next chapter would bring.

> "*Embrace the chaos; it's where the magic of life truly happens.*"
>
> – *Unknown*

Chennai, 2011

Wings of Change

As Kiara stepped into the waiting area post security check-in, the vastness of the space overwhelmed her, resembling a bustling shopping mall with its multitude of stores and travelers. Bewildered, she found herself walking in circles, disoriented by the chaotic energy around her. The mess inside mirrored the tumult of her thoughts—anxiety about her work, the weight of her bag, and the overwhelming crowd, all compounded by a gnawing hunger that refused to be ignored.

"Everything here is absurdly expensive," she mumbled, a hint of frustration edging her voice. "It feels like every traveler is a millionaire! Even a cup of coffee costs Rs. 250!" As she scanned the menus of the various outlets, her irritation deepened. Determined to quell her hunger without breaking the bank, she settled on a modest packet of peanuts, filled her water bottle at a nearby station, and finally found a comfortable chair to rest her weary body. She set her bag aside but could not shake off the cloud of worry looming over her. The lines on her forehead deepened, and her wide-open eyes betrayed her lack of confidence. As she cracked open the peanuts and glanced up at the large screen displaying a flurry of departing flights, a wave of mixed emotions washed over her. Agreeing to work on a project that required travel had seemed exciting at first, but now the gravity of the situation weighed heavily on her. With Rehan on leave, she hesitated, contemplating whether to call him for reassurance. She knew he would likely be awake at this hour, and the thought of hearing his voice offered a flicker of comfort amid her uncertainty. Taking a deep breath, she reached for her phone, hoping it would ease her racing thoughts as she prepared for the journey ahead.

Rehan is quite a personality. Standing tall at around 5 feet 11 inches, with angular features and a fair complexion, he exuded an effortless charm that made him impossible to overlook. His physique was well-maintained, a result of both his natural build and his disciplined habits. Coming from a wealthy family, Rehan was the first among his cousins to pursue a degree in software engineering—most of them barely graduated, leaving him a clear standout in his family. His father owned a successful cotton garment business in Surat, Gujarat, and the paycheck from this job seemed like mere pocket money to him. Yet, despite his affluence, Rehan was the last person to flaunt it. His appearance was always immaculate, his demeanor uplifting, and his voice soft-spoken—traits that set him apart from the usual brash confidence of the privileged. In fact, he was arguably the politest person she had ever encountered in the workplace, never putting on airs despite the quiet wealth he carried. He had the dangerous combination of a baby face and an athletic build, which made him the dream of almost every woman at work. Yet, he wasn't interested in indulging in flirtations or attention; most of his female coworkers tried to get close to him, but he gently declined, never leading anyone on. Therefore, he possessed all the characteristics of being a boyfriend rather than a mere friend. The phone rang several times before Rehan finally picked up, his groggy voice drifting through the speaker.

"Helloooo," he muttered, clearly still half-asleep.

Kiara didn't waste any time. "Hey, listen," she began, her voice tight with anxiety, "I'm terribly afraid. A lot of strange thoughts are crossing my mind. How do I get rid of them? Do I really need to go? Is there any way I can say 'No' now?"

Rehan, now fully awake, stifled a smirk but kept his tone steady and reassuring. "Stay calm, Kiara. It's a fantastic opportunity for you to grow and learn. Of all the girls on our team, you're the most courageous. You're not just 'quite fine,' you can do so much more. Anytime you run into trouble, just ping me on Messenger. I'll be there to help you solve it."

Her nerves began to settle, a small sense of relief washing over her as his words sank in. The boarding announcement for passengers in Zone 3 crackled over the intercom, signalling the end of the call. "Thanks, Rehan," she said, her voice softer now, and added, "I'll talk to you soon."

A short while later, her phone buzzed. It was a message from Rehan: "I know you'll finish this project and return with flying colours."

Kiara smiled in response, her tension easing just a little more.

"Good morning, everyone! In five minutes, zone 2 passengers will begin boarding flight number 6E19 from New Delhi to Chennai," announced a pleasant voice over the loudspeaker. Her eyes flicked to the boarding gate as she joined the line with the other passengers. Her exhaustion weighed heavily on her, and all she wanted was to find her seat, close her eyes, and maybe catch a glimpse of the city below during take-off. As she reached her row, her heart sank when she realized her seat was the middle one. She double-checked her boarding pass, feeling a flicker of hope that perhaps she had made a mistake, but a quick glance at the man holding the aisle seat confirmed the truth. This was her seat.

"Madam! B stands for the middle seat," he remarked with a raised eyebrow. She merely nodded, accepting his odd look with a slight shrug. It was her first flight, after all—what did she know? To her surprise, the flight was packed. There wasn't a single empty seat. "Why do people get up so early?, she pondered," irritation flickering across her face as she scanned the packed cabin. Her initial excitement to record videos and take photos, to capture this moment of her first flight, disappeared in an instant. With a resigned sigh, she squeezed into the middle seat, wedged between two older passengers who seemed polite enough, though neither tried to engage. She adjusted herself as best as she could, bracing for the long flight ahead, and tried to ignore the discomfort as the plane began to taxi down the runway.

"Welcome to flight 6E19, ladies and gentlemen," the captain's voice crackled through the intercom. "This is your captain speaking."

While the other passengers fidgeted with their seat belts, adjusted their pillows, and tried to find a comfortable position in the cramped space, she remained alert, her mind racing. She couldn't shake the anxiety that seemed to settle in her chest. As the flight attendants began their safety demonstration, she listened closely, her eyes scanning the instructions on the instructions card in front of her. She wasn't taking anything for granted, not on her first flight. And then she overheard something that sent a chill down her spine. "In case of a water landing…"

She froze. "What?" Her mind struggled to process the words. This aircraft can land on water. The thought was absurd. She tried to picture it—the massive plane floating on the sea, stretching out in all directions, and passengers scrambling to evacuate through the tiny emergency exits. The image was unsettling, and a wave of unease washed over her. That must be dreadful, she thought, her heart racing as she imagined the chaos of such a scenario. She quickly tried to push the thought out of her mind, but it lingered, nagging at her as the flight continued to taxi down the runway.

"Ready for departure," the captain's voice announced, calm and clear.

Her anxiety soared as the aircraft began to taxi down the tarmac, slowly picking up speed in preparation for take-off. She tried to peer out the window to catch a glimpse of the runway, but the seat belt across her waist restricted her movement. She could barely see anything beyond the edge of the glass. Suddenly, the elderly woman sitting by the window turned toward her with a knowing smirk. "First time?" she asked, her eyes twinkling with amusement. Kiara blushed, nodding quickly. She hadn't realized she was so obvious. Without saying a word, she sank back into her seat, trying to ignore the discomfort of the hard cushion beneath her. The lights in the cabin were dimmed, and the hum of the engines filled the air. As the plane inched forward, the engines roared to life, and she felt the plane's slow acceleration against her body. The rush of movement pressed her back into the seat as the aircraft gained speed, and before she could fully register it, the wheels left the ground. With a smooth, almost effortless motion, the plane soared into the sky, leaving the city lights behind.

After a while, the lights in the cabin were switched on, and the flight attendants began to move about, attending to the passengers. She watched them in awe, unable to help herself. She tried to avoid staring directly at the Steward and hostess, but she couldn't help but be astounded by their beauty. How can people be so perfect? she wondered, a scowl forming on her face. They're lucky that God has given them such exquisite looks. As the flight progressed, her discomfort grew. She was squeezed between two passengers, both unknowingly pushing her hands onto the shared armrest. She started to feel claustrophobic. After a few minutes of being uncomfortable, she pressed the call button for assistance.

"I'm feeling a bit dizzy. Is there any chance there's a spare aisle seat available?"

The air hostess, ever composed, nodded without a flicker of irritation. "Let me check, ma'am," she said politely before walking away. Her heart raced with anticipation. She just needed a little extra space.

A few minutes later, the flight attendant returned with good news. "We've got a seat for you in the first row of economy class, with more legroom." Kiara's joy was unmistakable. She settled into her new seat, a satisfied grin spreading across her face. Closing her eyes, she put the chaos of her day behind her. The turbulence of the moment faded as she relaxed into the comfort of her newfound space. All you need to do is let go and fly, she thought, a smile playing on her lips. The pieces of the puzzle will eventually fit together on their own.

And so, a new chapter in Kiara's life began.

Chennai, 2011

First Impressions

The flight made a smooth landing, and she felt a wave of relief wash over her as the aircraft touched down. She followed the flow of passengers, exiting the plane and heading toward conveyor belt number 7, as announced during the flight. The bustling crowd gathered around the belt, and she joined them, eagerly waiting for her luggage. As the bags began to appear, she noticed that some of the bags on the conveyor looked exactly like hers. Red luggage with a hard top seemed to be the trend at that moment, and in the sea of identical bags, she felt a flicker of panic. Slowly, the crowd began to filter out, each person lining up to pick up their respective bags. She had been waiting for some time, and as she plugged in her headphones, humming softly to herself, she thought she saw a woman in the crowd walking away with her bag. Kiara froze, her body going cold. She couldn't speak, couldn't move—her eyes locked on the woman, who was casually strolling away with the red suitcase. Was that my bag? The thought made her stomach churn. She wanted to stop the woman, to confront her and ask if the bag was hers, but the fear of looking foolish held her back. What if it wasn't hers? What if she made a scene for nothing? As the seconds ticked by, she noticed there were more and more bags of the same color and style. They all looked the same from a distance. Anxiety began to claw at her, especially when, one by one, the people around her picked up bags with the same hard red top. Minutes felt like hours, and as she stood there, her nerves building, the crowd around her slowly thinned. Twenty-five minutes passed, and then, finally, there it was—her red suitcase, appearing on the belt. She exhaled a breath she hadn't realized she was holding. She recognized it instantly, the Eiffel Tower sticker she had carefully placed on it the night before now clearly visible on the hard top. She was likely the last person to grab their bag, but it didn't matter. She took it, gathered her belongings, and walked out of the baggage claim area, her mind still racing but relieved to have the right bag in hand.

As Kiara crossed the exit gate, her once-bright smile quickly faded into a tight, stern frown. The air outside hit her like a wall—thick with dust, smoke, and an unbearable humidity that seemed to wrap around her body. The sudden rush of heat nearly pushed her right back inside the cool confines of the airport. She lifted her hand to her glasses, but they had already fogged up, leaving her momentarily blind to the scene before her. The sweat began to bead on her forehead, and soon, she was drenched from head to toe. For a split second, a thought crossed her mind: Why not turn back? The longing for the comfort of home, of familiarity, was so strong it almost made her step back. But she squashed the urge, focusing on the task at hand. Her mind was a whirlwind of conflicting emotions—excitement, dread, delight, and fear—each vying for her attention. Yet, amidst the chaos, one thought rose to the surface: Logistics. She paused and breathed in, striving to regain her composure. Looking around, she realized she was standing at the threshold of a new chapter in her life. Taxi drivers stood in neat rows with placards in hand, waiting for their respective passengers. Most of them likely came from the city's upscale hotels, ready to chauffeur visitors around the bustling streets. The scene felt so ordinary. So different from the dream she'd once had. She had always imagined this moment differently. She had often dreamed of a charming young man standing at the airport, waiting for her with a bouquet of flowers, a platinum ring in hand, and the promise of a fairy-tale proposal. She'd imagined the romance of it all, like the classic jazz scenes in old movies—glamorous, perfect. But reality was nothing like that. Instead of a dashing prince to sweep her off her feet, there was a driver standing awkwardly with a placard that spelled her name wrong—Kiarah—the extra "h" grating on her nerves. She loathed the way her name looked on paper when it was altered like that. With a reluctant sigh, she waved at the driver. He approached, nodded politely, and without a word, began loading her luggage into the car's boot. The excitement that had filled her moments before now seemed distant and small, overshadowed by the mundane reality of the situation. And so, her journey in this new city began—not with a magical, fairy-tale moment, but with the quiet hum of the car as it pulled away from the airport.

Even though she thought of exploring the city, immersing herself in its rich Tamil traditions and culture, the intense heat immediately made her second-guess her decision. The relentless humidity and sweltering temperatures were unbearable, and she found herself questioning whether she could endure this level of discomfort for long. When she arrived at the hotel, hoping for a bit of respite, her spirits sank further. She had assumed that, given the prestigious client she was working with, the company would have booked her into at least a 4-star hotel—if not a 5-star luxury one. But instead, the project manager had reserved a room at a modest guest house. The real blow came when she realized the guest house was located directly opposite Sheraton, a lavish hotel that seemed to mock her humble accommodation. As she trudged inside, led by a housekeeping staff member, her disappointment seemed to compound with every step. But once she entered the room, her sense of frustration began to dissipate, albeit slightly. It wasn't much, but it was a relief compared to what she had feared. The room, while modest, was pleasant in its own way. A queen-size bed made of rustic wood sat in the center of the room, covered with immaculate creamy white linens. The space smelled of jasmine and lilies, thanks to a soothing aroma diffuser. A lamp in the corner emitted a soft, warm glow, creating a peaceful, almost romantic ambiance. The overall aesthetic was modern, vibrant, and simple—nothing extravagant, but clean and pleasant. The room was a perfect fit for her minimalist tastes. It wasn't luxurious, but in that moment, it felt like a drop of cool water in a desert.

After a quick breakfast of juice and a sandwich, she changed into her work clothes with renewed energy, ready to tackle the day ahead. By the time she made her way to the office, the afternoon sun was already high, signalling that half the day had slipped by. After a few frustrating moments of trying to locate the building and gain access, she finally made her way to her project manager's desk. As she hurried through the corridors, she caught a glimpse of Venkat through a glass-panelled conference room door. He was in the middle of what seemed to be another meeting. Venkat wasn't tall—standing at only about 5 feet 5 inches—but his presence was commanding, nonetheless. He had wheatish skin, large glasses perched on his nose, and a thick Mustache that seemed to enhance his already prominent features. His protruding stomach made him look more amusing than intimidating from an appearance standpoint, but it was his actions that truly defined him.

Venkat was known for his sharp intellect, and his reputation as one of the smartest project managers at the company was well earned. He was highly regarded for his ability to manage projects with precision, combining both the art and science of project management. But in that moment, she could tell he was agitated. He was gesturing wildly with his hands, his voice rising with frustration. From the looks of it, he was having a heated discussion with someone inside the conference room. She quickly retreated to her desk, not wanting to interrupt. As she was going through her emails, her phone rang. It was Venkat calling.

"Join me in the conference room," he instructed curtly.

Kiara, somewhat surprised, stood up and made her way to the conference room. When she entered, she was taken aback to find two of her colleagues already seated in the room, both looking visibly frustrated and emotionally drained. They were around her age, all new to the company, and clearly, this assignment was their first real challenge as well. Venkat didn't look like he was in the mood for any pleasantries.

"I assume you all know each other. No need for introductions," Venkat said bluntly. "Let's get to the point. I'm sure your team leads in Gurgaon have briefed you on the product delivery, and you've all been asked to prepare a presentation on your approach and understanding of the project. I see you have your laptops, so connect to the projector and start presenting, one at a time."

Venkat didn't waste time with niceties or small talk. He was all business, and the room fell into a tense silence. Each of her colleagues began their presentation, but it was clear from the start that none of them had a real understanding of the subject matter. The project was complex, and they were all caught off guard. None of them were able to explain things adequately. They stumbled through their slides, their voices shaking with uncertainty. Venkat didn't interrupt, but she could feel his simmering frustration. When the last presentation finished, the room fell silent again. Then, as though the dam had broken, Venkat erupted. "What the hell was that? Do you find this funny? You have no idea how the customer's system works. I don't even know why you were hired in the first place!" His voice echoed off the walls, sharp and unforgiving. The sting of his words was palpable. Kiara observed the situation unfold and understood that she needed to act quickly. This was her chance to prove herself—not just to Venkat, but to everyone in the room. Her confidence was the only thing she had to rely on. Even if she didn't know all the details, she couldn't afford to show weakness. After all, this wasn't the first time she had been put on the spot. She'd had moments in the past where she had to fake it until she made it. This was no different. When her turn came, she connected her laptop to the projector. Her hands were steady, her voice calm, and though her mind raced to find the right words, she spoke with authority. Her presentation was flawless—not because she had all the answers, but because she delivered her information with such conviction that it appeared as though she had a deep understanding of the project. Her confidence, her poise, the way she structured her thoughts—all of it worked in her favour. Venkat, who had been silent throughout her presentation, leaned back in his chair. She could sense his approval, though he remained stoic. When she finished, he gave a short nod and said, "Choosing you for this assignment was the right call."

Kiara exhaled, feeling the weight lift off her shoulders. She had managed to impress Venkat, and in doing so, she had secured her place in the project. For the first time since arriving in the city, she felt a glimmer of confidence that maybe, just maybe, she was ready for this challenge. Venkat got a call, and he left the room in an eerie silence, and the momentary relief felt by her and her coworkers was palpable. They both smiled at her, offering words of praise for her well-delivered presentation. But despite their praise, she couldn't shake the feeling that something was off. She had sensed when Venkat patted her back, a gesture that felt too public, too calculated. It was as if he had intentionally placed her on a pedestal, not for her benefit, but to alienate her from the rest of the team. As she sat back down at her desk, she tried to push the thoughts aside. She had been a part of the team for only a few hours, and she didn't want to jump to conclusions. But she couldn't ignore the growing sense of unease gnawing at her. The more she thought about it, the more she realized that something about the way Venkat had singled her out felt off. She had been praised in front of everyone, sure, but that kind of praise often came with strings attached strings that could quickly turn into knots if one wasn't careful.

She had arrived in Chennai with dreams of discovering its vibrant culture, its bustling streets, and the picturesque beaches. However, reality quickly set in. Her work, always her top priority, began to consume her time and energy. The city's allure faded into the background as the urgency of her project took center stage. Needing a moment to herself, she took a break and headed to the cafeteria. The sight that greeted her, however, made her feel out of place. People were eating with their hands, mixing rice, curd, and daal in ways that seemed completely foreign to her. She tried to focus on buying herself a meal and deciding to play it safe, she chose Anna and Sambar, the familiar combination of rice and lentils from her northern roots. To her surprise, the dish was both comforting and delicious. She found herself appreciating the simplicity of the food. There was something undeniably satisfying about it—a lesson in the beauty of simplicity that she hadn't expected to learn. Days passed and she kept on exploring different South Indian dishes. However, the mounting challenges at work each day, made her feel increasingly isolated. The project she had been assigned seemed more daunting by the day, and despite reaching out for help, she found little support from her peers and superiors back in Gurgaon. Her attempts to contact them were met with silence or dismissive replies.

"Even your shadow leaves you in darkness," she thought bitterly, feeling abandoned in a city that, at first, had seemed so full of promise.

To make matters worse, her manager Arjun, who had once been a trusted ally, now criticized her for not being able to handle even the simplest tasks. The harsh words stung. The confident Kiara who had come to Chennai feeling capable now felt lost and unsure of herself. But she refused to give in. She was no stranger to challenges and had always pushed herself beyond her limits. This time, she decided to take control. She methodically listed the problems she was facing and identified the gaps in her knowledge. She revisited the materials she had downloaded, ran tests on the sandbox systems, and read countless online articles to find solutions. It wasn't easy—there were many sleepless nights and moments of frustration—but over time, she began to understand the complexities of the project. Slowly, she was mastering the system, learning more about both the product and the people she worked with. As the deadline approached, the pressure mounted. Her days had become a blur of code, configurations, and endless problem-solving. She regretted not having taken the opportunity to explore, but there was no turning back now. The project had to be completed. Though she was exhausted, she had learned to adapt. The setbacks had made her stronger, more resilient. And when she finally delivered the project, she would know that she had earned her place, not only in Chennai, but in her own eyes. The journey may not have been what she had expected, but it had taught her the value of perseverance and self-reliance. And in the end, that was all that mattered.

Being a Scorpio, her restless nature constantly drove her to dive into a multitude of interests—poetry, music, photography, and anything else that sparked her curiosity. But lately, it felt like her passion for life was being slowly drained by the weight of her project. The demands of work consumed her, leaving little room for anything else. Yet, one fine evening, she made up her mind: she would reclaim a piece of herself, even if just for a short while.

Determined to visit Marina Beach, she set off around 5:00 p.m. The sun was dipping low, casting a warm orange glow over the skyline. The temperature had dropped from the sweltering heat of the day, and the clouds were rolling in, hinting at a storm. She had hoped for company, but none of her friends were free. Undeterred, Kiara made her way to the beach alone. The beach was less crowded than usual for a weekday, with only a few locals scattered along the stretch of golden sand. The rhythm of the ocean's waves crashing against the shore was soothing, and the cool breeze felt like a relief from the stifling office air. She smiled, feeling the sand squish beneath her toes as she walked along the coastline, humming softly to herself. The feeling was pure freedom. As the waves reached her feet, she couldn't resist the childish joy of running backward every time they brushed her skin. The simple act of playing in the surf made her laugh, and for the first time in days, she felt relieved and grateful for the quiet pleasure of the moment. As she continued walking, her eyes caught a glint of something in the sand—a perfect conch, partially buried. She knelt, brushing away the sand, her fingers tracing its smooth spiral. It was beautiful, the intricate ridges and smooth surface almost hypnotic. She rinsed it gently in the sea, her mind marvelling at the craftsmanship of nature.

"Should I try blowing it?" she wondered. She hesitated, the thought of hygiene crossing her mind. "I'm not sure if it's clean," she muttered to herself, but the pull of curiosity was stronger. The conch seemed to call to her.

Before she could bring it to her lips, the sky suddenly darkened, and the first raindrops began to fall. She laughed as the rain started to pour down in torrents, drenching her in an instant. There was something refreshing about the cool rain on her skin. She stuck out her tongue, tasting the drops as they fell from the sky. The feeling of the rain on her face, so simple and pure, made her smile. For a fleeting moment, she wanted to abandon all reason and dance freely in the rain, spinning and laughing without a care in the world. But she refrained and walked back slowly towards the guesthouse, enjoying the sound of the rain on the ground and the rhythmic pulse of the ocean in the distance. As she passed by, she slipped the conch into her purse, trying to hide her grin. There was something mischievous about it, as though she were stealing a secret from nature itself. By the time she reached the guesthouse, she was soaked through. Her hair clung to her face, and she couldn't stop sneezing from the chill. Still, there was a warmth in her heart, a sense of contentment she hadn't felt in days. The rain had washed away more than just the dust of the day; it had washed away the heaviness of her worries, if only for a little while.

Manoj, the guesthouse staff, was one of those rare souls whose kindness seemed boundless. A native of Varanasi, a city steeped in history and spirituality, he had faced his own share of life's unpredictability. His dreams of becoming an engineer had been shattered when his father passed away, and with limited formal education—only up to class 10—he had set out to support himself. Following the advice of a cousin, he had come to Chennai, hoping to find work. Life, it seemed, had its own plans for him, steering him down a path he hadn't anticipated. When he saw her drenched from the rain, a sense of concern immediately crossed his face. Without a word from her, he went straight to work, preparing a steaming cup of tea for her. It was a gesture so simple yet profoundly thoughtful that Kiara felt an unexpected warmth wash over her. As she gratefully accepted the tea, she couldn't help but smile. "Thank you," she said softly, appreciating the small yet significant act of kindness. Manoj, with his ever-present humility, blushed and replied, "No problem." His quiet generosity was a reminder of the humanity that still exists in the world, a balm for Kiara's worn-out spirit. After sipping her tea, feeling the warmth seep into her body, she stood up to return to her room. As she walked down the corridor, a small detail caught her attention—a "Do Not Disturb" sign hung on the door next to hers which signified that someone else had checked into the guesthouse, and for the first time since her arrival, she was no longer the only guest on the floor. It might have seemed like an insignificant change, but for her, it was a relief. Her thoughts momentarily drifted to the unfamiliarity of the past few days—the isolation, the overwhelming work, and the challenges she'd faced in her new environment. Now, with the presence of another guest, the sense of solitude that had accompanied her began to lift, like the cloudiness that had followed her earlier in the day. She returned to her room, her heart a little lighter, knowing that life, in all its unpredictability, sometimes brought moments of kindness and change when they were needed most.

The next morning, with a warm smile, Manoj brought Kiara her breakfast, the tray carefully balanced in his hands as he knocked softly on her door. "Good morning, Ma'am! How are you feeling today?" he asked, his voice laced with concern.

"I'm good, bhaiya," she replied cheerfully, her tiredness momentarily forgotten as she returned his smile. She waved him off, thanking him as he left her to enjoy the meal in peace. After he left, she quickly dressed, eager to get started on the day ahead. While enjoying her breakfast, she couldn't find the newspaper. She'd grown accustomed to reading it every morning, especially the comic and fashion columns. It had become a comforting routine, a small escape from the pressures of work and the loneliness she sometimes felt. No matter how busy she was, she'd always sneak a peek, enjoying the snippets of what's happening in the world. She decided to head outside to the patio in search of the paper. As she stepped out, she spotted a man sitting in a corner, deeply engrossed in the very newspaper she sought. With a playful smile and a pleading look on her face, she asked, "Excuse me, could I borrow the newspaper for a moment?" The man glanced up at her, his irritation evident from the interruption.

However, as he met her eyes, he hesitated. She gave him a slightly exaggerated, pleading expression, and with a sigh, he relented, handing her the newspaper. Kiara beamed with gratitude and skipped back to her room, holding it like a small victory. What she didn't realize was that the man was staring at her, utterly taken aback by her carefree energy and enthusiasm, his jaw nearly dropping as she danced away with the paper in hand. After finishing her breakfast, she quickly brushed her hair, trying to get ready as quickly as possible. The cab downstairs was waiting, and she knew that the driver wouldn't tolerate being kept waiting for more than a couple of minutes. "Phew! What a challenging person!" She whispered to herself with a grin as she hurried out of the room. As she passed through the lobby to leave the guest house, she caught sight of the same man she had borrowed the newspaper from, still sitting on the sofa, his face hidden behind a book. He was so engrossed in his reading that he barely noticed her walking by. She paused for a moment, wondering about him. Was he here for business? For leisure? "Who cares!" she laughed, brushing it off. "I've got a world to save!" she joked to herself; her mood lightened by her own playful thoughts. With that, she stepped out into the day, her energy renewed and ready for whatever came next.

The cab driver's constant grumbling had become a regular part of her daily routine. As he yelled at her for being late again, she simply nodded in response, not letting his bad mood affect hers. She'd long since grown accustomed to his abrasive attitude. He was perpetually cranky, always in a rush, and never tried to communicate clearly. Despite his sour demeanour, she had learned to tune him out. She focused instead on the task at hand—the long ride to the office, which, though annoying, gave her precious time to work. She plugged in her headphones and opened the laptop. The way to the office became her unofficial study session. As the cab bumped along the road, she immersed herself in the knowledge base, searching for answers to her ever-growing list of questions. Her resolve to minimize knowledge gaps and dependencies drove her to make the most of every available moment. The more problems she encountered, the more she learned. Soon, she was breezing through the materials, reading and absorbing information at an incredible pace. What had started as a mere survival tactic—trying to stay afloat in a sea of new knowledge—had turned into a passion. She began to see herself as a walking, talking encyclopaedia, able to quote articles, solve technical problems, and answer questions without hesitation. Even subject matter specialists, who had spent years honing their expertise, were sometimes taken aback by how quickly she grasped complex concepts. Her persistence began to pay off. She stopped waiting for others to give her answers. She no longer depended on her superiors for guidance or validation; instead, she trusted her own instincts and skills. She learned how to fix problems on her own, sometimes even before her colleagues realized there was an issue. Her transformation didn't go unnoticed. The people around her began to rely on her more and more, and their trust in her grew exponentially. Venkat, ever eager to boast, was no exception. He would frequently praise her to his superiors, saying, "When I interviewed her, I knew she had potential. You see, I have a knack for spotting talent." While he might have wanted to take some credit, she knew that the real credit belonged to her relentless effort and her passion for learning.

Through it all, she had learned an important lesson: hard work truly has no substitute. It wasn't about luck or shortcuts; it was and is always about dedication and perseverance.

Chennai, 2011

A surprising invitation

Kiara lay back on the bed, a pillow cradling her head and another wedged between her knees. The soft hum of the air conditioning, the calming scent of lavender from the diffuser, and the flicker of white candlelight created an atmosphere of peace. As she reflected on her progress, the people around her, and the obstacles she had overcome with nothing but her grit and determination, she felt a deep sense of satisfaction. She had come so far—and yet, there was still so much to navigate. But her thoughts were suddenly broken by a knock at the door. The sound shattered the stillness, pulling her out of her reverie. She groaned quietly, unwilling to move from the comfort of the bed. She glanced at the clock on the bedside table: 7:15 p.m. Expecting it to be the housekeeping staff delivering her dinner, she threw on a weary expression and walked to the door. To her surprise, it wasn't the staff but the man from next door. He stood in the doorway, holding a tray filled with food. His deep, rich voice filled the space as he asked, "Would you kindly accompany me to the dining room?"

She hesitated, unsure whether she wanted to leave her cozy sanctuary, but the thought of a quiet meal alone made her reconsider. She hadn't realized how much she needed some form of interaction, a little break from her own thoughts. After a pause, she smiled softly and walked towards the dinner table. The man was undeniably attractive—tall, dark, and handsome in the classic Indian sense, with an effortless charisma that could make any woman stop in her tracks. His voice had that deep, resonant quality that made even the simplest sentences seem compelling. He wore a crisp white shirt tucked into well-fitted blue Levi's jeans—a combination that was impossible to go wrong with. His unkempt beard and the salt-and-pepper hair, tousled just so, added a rugged charm that was impossible to ignore.

With an earnest smile, he introduced himself. "Hi, I'm Sameer, and I'm from Mumbai."

Kiara smiled back, surprised by his easy confidence.

"Hey, I'm Kiara."

"Are you here for work or leisure?"

"I'm here for work," she responded. "I'm here for my first assignment, and I'm happy that it's going to end soon. Just one more month and I can finally go back home."

As they continued to talk, her initial disinterest and irritation melted away. Sameer's warmth and easy conversation put her at ease. She began to forget that she was dressed in her nightwear, feeling a little awkward at first, but quickly realizing that it didn't seem to matter to him. In fact, as the conversation deepened, she could tell that Sameer was more interested in who she was than in what she was wearing. What she didn't know was that he had been just as captivated by her as she was by him. What had truly floored him were her dimples, the way they appeared when she smiled. It was that simple, infectious charm that drew him in. Through their conversation, she learned that Sameer was also on a short-term assignment in Chennai, just like her. He was a project manager who would be leaving in a month, too. What really clicked between them was their shared love for reading and sports. They discovered that they both enjoyed books and had a particular fondness for them.

Curious, Sameer asked, "So, what kind of books do you like to read?"

Her eyes lit up with enthusiasm. "I love romantic novels!" she said, her voice full of excitement. She could talk for hours about her favourite genres and authors, and the conversation seemed to flow effortlessly from there.

"I believe romantic stories are often disconnected from real life. Don't you agree?"

She was astonished by his question because she hadn't anticipated it.

"Reading gives everyone wings of imagination, and reading about such genre makes me more inclined to believe in love. It gives everyone an access to a world of fairytales that is very different from our monotonous, hectic lives. It allows us to breathe. It allows us to live a thousand lives before we die."

His jaw dropped, and for a moment, he was left speechless. The way Kiara spoke about her love for romantic novels, the passion in her voice, made him rethink everything he had ever thought about the genre. Though he'd never been drawn to romantic fiction himself, the depth of emotion she expressed made him feel an unexpected pull. Maybe, just maybe, he thought, he needed to start reading them again with a fresh perspective. The realization hit him that it wasn't just the content of the books that intrigued her, but the way they connected her to a world of feelings and stories, something he could appreciate. Their conversation lasted for what felt like an endless stream of words, both sharing pieces of themselves that they hadn't expected to reveal so easily. It was one of those rare, effortless exchanges where time seemed to lose all meaning. Eventually, the night grew late, and they parted ways, retreating to their respective rooms. As she lay on her bed later, reflecting on their time together, a sense of relief washed over her. There was something about him—his easy confidence, his genuine interest—that had helped her shed some of the walls she had carefully built around herself. She thought about the way she had always kept to herself, seeing it as "me time," the solitude that she had convinced herself was necessary. But now, lying in the quiet of her room, she realized that the solitude she clung to was not the healthy, restorative space she had always believed it to be.

"Me time," she mused, "is just a self-limiting belief." It wasn't really a way to nurture oneself; it was a way to stay stuck. She had been embracing loneliness, convincing herself that being alone was the only path to self-discovery. But tonight, she saw things differently. Maybe true growth came not from isolation but from opening up to others, from sharing experiences, from allowing herself to be vulnerable. The thought left her with a strange sense of hope, and for the first time in a long while, she felt ready to let more people in.

The following day, a subtle change began to unfold between both. They started sharing meals together, and what began as simple exchanges slowly evolved into something more. They would talk about anything and everything under the sun, from their childhood memories to their dreams for the future. There was no topic too trivial or too serious for them to explore. Every conversation felt natural, effortless, and honest. Each would listen intently, accepting the other's viewpoint without judgment, and offering their own without hesitation. It was a rare and refreshing kind of connection. They soon realized how much they enjoyed each other's company. Their conversations were filled with laughter and light-heartedness, each moment leaving them feeling lighter and more understood. There was an ease between them that allowed them to speak openly, say what they felt without overthinking, and simply enjoy being in each other's presence. It was the kind of connection that made the world outside seem less important, as if time itself would stop whenever they were together.

It was the last working day of the month; she was in a rush. After finishing her tasks, she quickly headed to the guesthouse, eager to drop off her laptop before heading out for a shopping trip with a colleague. As she entered the guesthouse and walked through the living room, she noticed Sameer sitting with his evening tea. He looked up when he heard her footsteps. Their gazes locked, and in that instant, an unspoken connection formed between them. It wasn't just a glance—it was a gaze that lingered, holding a silent, yet powerful connection. Kiara felt an unexpected flutter in her chest, a rapid pulse she hadn't anticipated. Her heart raced, and a tingling sensation spread down her spine. She felt oddly parched, like her throat had gone dry, and as she tried to make sense of it, she found herself unable to look away. It was as though the world had slowed, the air between them thick with unspoken emotion. She glanced down, trying to compose herself, but her mind raced. Why was her body reacting this way? What was it about this moment, this gaze, that made her heart pound faster than usual? She didn't understand it, but she couldn't deny it. There was something stirring inside her—a feeling that was both unfamiliar and strangely exhilarating.

"Hello," Kiara said, her attention slightly elsewhere as she entered the living room.

"Hey, all good? Is something out of place?" he asked, looking up from his tea with a curious expression.

"Yeah, everything's alright," she responded a little too fast.

"I'm glad to hear that. Are you in a hurry? You seem a bit restless!"

"No, I'm fine," she assured him, offering a faint smile.

"Are you heading somewhere?" he asked, intrigued by her sudden shift in energy.

"Yeah, to the mall with a colleague. I'll see you later."

With that, she quickly excused herself and dashed off to her room. Before he could say anything else, she was already out of the living room, and he watched her retreat with a puzzled expression. Why was she behaving so strangely? he wondered, before heading back to his own room, a thought lingering in his mind. As for Kiara, she found herself unexpectedly giddy. There was something about the way he had looked at her that made her heart race a little faster. She liked the way he saw her—perhaps more than she realized. After freshening up, she opened her closet and settled on a printed black dress, elegant but simple, with a silver silk scarf tied in a bow around her neck. A pair of black heels and silver earrings added the finishing touches. As she looked at herself in the full-length mirror, she couldn't help but smile. She pointed at her reflection in the mirror and said, "You look great, girl, but you know what will make you look even better? A new outfit."

It was a small, fun moment, but it made her feel good—like she was taking control, not just of her appearance, but of the way she was beginning to embrace the unexpected, including the growing connection with

Sameer. She hurriedly left her room, hoping to catch a glimpse of Sameer in the patio, but by the time she stepped out, he was nowhere to be seen. She could feel a pang of disappointment gnawing at her, and despite her best efforts to shake it off, thoughts of him lingered in her mind as she made her way to the mall. The weight of her emotions felt like an anchor she couldn't quite escape. On the drive to the mall, her coworker Priya hummed a tune, seemingly unaware of Kiara's distracted mood. The mall was a typical Friday madhouse, bustling with payday shoppers, each in a hurry to snap up their weekend purchases. But Kiara couldn't focus on any of it. Without much thought, Priya dragged her into one of her favourite stores, a high-end boutique filled with clothing from various illustrious Indian designers. Kiara tried to lose herself in the first rack of clothes she saw, selecting a few pieces to try on. But as soon as she stepped into the fitting room, the nagging thoughts of Sameer crept back in, making her feel restless and frustrated. Her reflection in the mirror appeared to taunt her. She hated that she couldn't shake off the thoughts of him. And then, the prices of the dresses she had picked out only added to her frustration. I can't afford to treat myself, she thought, feeling a mix of guilt and helplessness. Unable to even try on the clothes, she left the outfits in the fitting room, feeling more deflated with every passing second. She waited for Priya, who eventually emerged from her own shopping frenzy in a whirlwind of clothes. After trying on several outfits, Priya had finally narrowed it down to two, with Kiara's input guiding her choices. Once they left the store, Priya insisted on stopping at their favourite dessert spot, hoping to lift Kiara's spirits with something sweet. As they dug into their treats, Kiara's thoughts were still far away. Priya, ever observant, noticed that her friend wasn't as upbeat as usual.

"Kiara," Priya said gently, breaking the silence, "you've been really quiet today. What's on your mind?"

Kiara looked up from her dessert, forcing a smile. She didn't want to burden Priya with her inner turmoil, but she also couldn't deny the weight on her chest. Why can't I stop thinking about him? she wondered silently.

"Are you okay?" Priya asked, noticing Kiara's quiet demeanour.

"Yeah. I'm good. Shall we go back?" Kiara flashed a brief smile, eager to escape the mall.

"Okay, let's go."

"Can you drive? I'm feeling exhausted," she said, massaging her temples.

"Yes, absolutely!" Priya answered, taking the keys.

The ride back to the guest house felt endless to Kiara. All she could think about was the conversation with Sameer and how his words had affected her more than she cared to admit. The drive was quiet, and even though Priya was talking along the way, Kiara's mind was a million miles away. When she finally arrived back at the guest house, she was eager to see him again. "I wonder if he's still around," she thought as she walked toward her room. And just as fate would have it, she spotted him heading toward the patio. She couldn't resist smiling as she observed him. There was something magnetic about him, and in that moment, she felt her gaze stick to him like glue.

"Hello. How did the shopping go?" he called out as he noticed her.

She scowled playfully, her lips curling into a small pout.

"Ah, I understand. How could it be fun without me?"

"By the way, you never told me that your friend was that attractive. I would have loved to go shopping with her."

Kiara raised an eyebrow. "Should I let her know?"

"Well, gracias. I'm kidding," he replied with a wink.

"I wish you wake up smiling in the morning," he added, smiling warmly as he turned to head out for dinner.

She stood there, feeling a rush of emotions—joy mixed with something else, something she couldn't quite identify. She smiled back and whispered, "Goodnight." But as he walked away, she suddenly felt a wave of emptiness wash over her. The smile on her face quickly faded as she questioned her own feelings. Why did that sting? she wondered. His words hadn't been cruel, but for some reason, they left her feeling unsettled. She shook her head, attempting to dismiss it. It's just a harmless joke, Kiara. Why is it bothering you so much? But her inner voice mocked her. When we don't understand why we feel the way we do, it's always uncomfortable. And sometimes, it can be a little frightening, don't you think? That night, as she lay awake in the bed, sleep eluded her. Thoughts of Sameer and his words danced in her mind, keeping her awake longer than she would have liked. What's happening to me? she pondered. He's just a friend. Why does this feel like more?

The next morning, she tried to arrive at work earlier than usual. She convinced herself that keeping her distance from Sameer would help her focus better. The idea of avoiding him felt like the right thing to do, even though a small part of her didn't want to. As she walked into the office, she meticulously planned her tasks for the day, determined to stay productive and stay on track. By 2:30 p.m., after finishing her tasks and sending her daily status reports, she rushed to leave.

"If you don't move faster, Anna, I'll be terribly late!" she called to the cab driver. The roads were unusually quiet as she travelled back to the guest house. Arriving at the guest house, she rushed to her room, quickly switching on the TV and tuning into Star Sports. The Indian cricket team was playing against Australia, and the match was crucial—it would determine whether India would make it to the 2011 World Cup semifinals. Cricket had always been a passion of hers, and the excitement was palpable. No matter how old you are, your obsession with the game remains as vivid as ever. And Cricket as a sport unites the country because blue blood runs through our veins, she thought, as she changed into a blue t-shirt and shorts to match the Indian cricket team's uniform.

Her heart raced with the thrill of the game ahead, and for a moment, all thoughts of Sameer were forgotten. The match was about to begin, and nothing could pull her away from the action.

> "*You don't have to go through it alone, just stay busy enough that you don't have time to think about them.*"
>
> *– Unknown*

Chennai, 2011

The World Cup

The match was in full swing, and Kiara's excitement reached fever pitch. As the Indian batsmen scored boundaries, she leapt up and down on her bed, her enthusiasm contagious, as if she were right there in the stadium. Every boundary was met with a loud cheer, and every sixer sent her into a frenzy of joy. Her body language mirrored that of someone playing the game themselves—pacing, gesturing, and shouting commands to the TV screen as though the players could hear her.

"Hit the ball hard! Aim for a sixer!" she yelled, her hands gesturing dramatically as if guiding the batsmen from her room. The adrenaline rush was palpable as she watched the match unfold. Her love for the game was evident in every word she spoke.

"You've got this, guys! It's an easy match!" she announced with confidence, as though she had an insider view of the game. The thrill of the moment surged through her, and nothing could tear her away from the action. Then, a knock at the door shattered her focus. She turned toward the door with a deep frown, annoyed at the interruption. She was so absorbed in the game that the thought of missing even a second of it was unbearable.

"Get lost!" she yelled in frustration, yet the knocking persisted. With a sigh and a growl of irritation, she finally walked over to open the door. To her surprise, it was Sameer standing on the other side.

"What happened? Why are you knocking on the door continuously?" she asked, her voice higher than usual, clearly still irked.

Sameer looked uncomfortable, his body language betraying his unease. "Could you turn off the television and come outside?" his voice nervous, his fists clenched. There was an air of tension about him, and his hesitance was palpable.

She raised her eyebrows in confusion, her frustration mixing with concern.

"Are you okay?" she asked, her arms folded as she watched him warily.

"Yeah. I am." His voice was quiet, but the nervous energy surrounding him said otherwise.

She looked at him for a moment, unconvinced. "Okay. If you say so, but looking at your face, it's hard to believe you." She softened her tone, still unsure about his true state of mind.

"No, I'm fine," Sameer reassured her, though his eyes darted around, avoiding direct contact.

She sighed, still puzzled. "Okay, but why did you want me to turn off the television? If I remember correctly, you said you liked tennis and cricket when we were chatting.

Why aren't you watching the game? Don't you want to watch this real tussle?"

Sameer shifted uncomfortably before responding. "Oh yeah, I'm a big fan, but… this is a big game—the quarterfinals. It's a nervous moment… at least for me."

He let out a deep breath, his words betraying the weight of the moment. "For me, it's a nerve-wracking rollercoaster ride that will test my patience and our team's mettle," he added, a hint of vulnerability in his voice.

She continued to look at him, the intensity of her gaze catching him off guard. She realized that, despite his calm exterior, he was just as invested in the game as she was. He wasn't just watching; he was feeling it.

"Alright," she said, her tone softening as she glanced back at the television. "I get it. But hey, we're both in this together, right? If we win, we win together. And if we lose…" She trailed off, offering a reassuring smile. "Well, we'll still be in this together."

He nodded, his expression softening a little. There was something unspoken between them now, something that went beyond just the game. It was a bond—small, yet significant.

Without saying much more, she turned off the television and followed him out to the patio, feeling a new kind of connection building. The game could wait, but this moment felt too important to ignore. Due to the widespread popularity of cricket across the globe, it had always been Kiara's favourite sport. Cricket was more than just a game to her—it was a reflection of life itself, teaching her about optimism, perseverance, and the power of staying grounded under pressure. She often thought about how life, much like cricket, had its own set of rules and strategies. The goal was to navigate through challenges, make the most of what you have, and remain focused on being the best version of yourself—just as a cricketer does on the field. She had grown up watching the game with an unmatched passion, absorbing every rule, every term, and every nuance of the sport. She understood the significance of each ball, every boundary, and every wicket. Cricket, for her, was more than a game—it was a metaphor for life. But as she looked at him, she realized something she had never witnessed before: he was panicking. His nervous energy, his clenched fists, and his uneasy body language during the game were unlike anything she had experienced with cricket. In her world, the game was a challenge to embrace, a test of patience, but Sameer seemed to be caught in the overwhelming weight of it all. Though she was used to feeling exhilarated by the highs and lows of the game, his anxiety made her realize just how differently people can experience the same thing. It made her think: life, like cricket, can be a series of unpredictable moments, but how we respond to them defines our journey. Some people thrive on pressure, while others may struggle. Just like in cricket, where a cool-headed batsman can turn the game around, the key to life's challenges lies in keeping calm, being adaptable, and trusting in your own abilities. She had learned that from years of watching cricket, but now, she was learning it from the way he was facing the game—perhaps even realizing that optimism isn't just about winning, but about how you play the game, no matter what the score might be. She sat at the dining table, her mind swirling with thoughts she couldn't quite articulate. The intensity with which some people clung to games; the unyielding passion that overshadowed everything else—it baffled her. She couldn't fathom the reasons, beyond national pride or the riches that often-followed victory. And yet, there was a strange fervour in it, an obsession she couldn't understand, and though it irritated her, she kept her thoughts to herself. Her gaze drifted toward Sameer, who had joined her, his presence unsettlingly calm yet charged with an energy that made the air seem thicker. He lowered himself into the chair, his foot tapping lightly, a subtle rhythm born of impatience, or perhaps something else altogether. She looked at him intently, her gaze unwavering, asking him to break the silence. But instead of speaking, he allowed a slow smile to spread across his face, the kind that seemed to hold secrets and quiet admiration. He glanced at her, his eyes catching hers just for a moment, lingering on her beauty, as if entranced by something he couldn't quite explain.

She tried to break the silence, her voice soft but persistent, hoping to draw him out of his restless state. Yet, Sameer could hardly sit still. He stood up abruptly, the chair scraping against the floor, and began pacing around the living room like a caged animal. The silence between them deepened, a space filled with the sound of his footfalls and the distant hum of the television. To his dismay, the living room wasn't an escape from the game that gnawed at him. One of the kitchen doors, which was conveniently located just beside him, led directly into the heart of the guesthouse. And inside, the staff were all gathered, their collective focus fixed on the screen. Despite the television being turned to the lowest volume, their voices, raised in exuberance and excitement, rippled through the air like an endless wave of noise. With every cheer, every shout, it felt as though the walls were closing in on him, amplifying his anxiety and heightening the simmering frustration within him. Unable to bear it any longer, he strode towards the door, throwing it open with a sharp motion.

"Quiet down!" he snapped at the staff, his voice laced with an edge of tension, as though the words themselves were a release for the pressure building inside him.

She watched him, her expression softening. A strange mix of pity and amusement swirled within her as she observed his plight. His behaviour, so childlike in its impulsive need to control the environment around him, both captivated and perplexed her. It was as if he were a child, throwing a tantrum because the world didn't bend to his will, and yet it was hard not to sympathize with him. His obsession with the match, his frantic desire to know every detail of every over, made him miserable—a desperation that clouded his every thought. It was like a hunger, a craving for something intangible, yet all-consuming. And yet, she couldn't help but see a reflection of herself in his agitation. She, too, was tethered to the match in her own way, wanting to Savor the thrill of it, yet unable to fully immerse herself in it because of the chaotic energy that surrounded them. Both, caught in a moment of shared discontent, each trapped in their own version of the same frustration. Kiara stood up from the chair, the weight of the situation pressing on her chest, and turned toward her room.

"Hey! Where are you headed? Stay with me here, please!" he called after her, his voice tinged with desperation, his feet shifting impatiently. She paused, turning just enough to catch his gaze, eyes wide with the soft spark of defiance, brows drawn together, her teeth clenched in silent frustration. She swallowed down her rising irritation, the words slipping out with a forced calm.

"I have to go to the restroom. May I?" she asked, her tone as steady as she could muster, though it was clear that she wanted nothing more than to escape the tight space of the living room and its unsettling noise.

"Of course," he replied, his voice soft but with an edge of unease that lingered between them.

Once she was alone in her room, she locked the door behind her, a small act of privacy she desperately needed. She hurried to the television, flicking it on as quickly as she could. The bright screen filled the space with life, offering a brief respite from the chaos. She tuned to the Sports channel, the familiar commentary offering her some sense of peace. A deep breath escaped her lips when she saw that Team India hadn't yet lost a player. She relaxed, sinking into the comfort of the match, savouring the full over she was now able to watch. The minutes passed in a blur as she caught up on the overs she had missed, her mind slowly unwinding with the game. Time slipped away unnoticed. What started as a brief escape stretched into twenty minutes of quiet solitude. The sudden knock on the door caught her off guard.

"How much longer, Ma'am?" Sameer's voice echoed, filled with impatience and a sense of urgency.

Quickly, Kiara turned off the television, the screen going dark as she opened the door to face him. His grin was wide, a playful mockery of her time spent alone.

"You sure spent a lot of time in there," he teased, a playful tone in his voice.

She couldn't resist smiling at him, catching a glimpse of his smile from the corner of her eye.

"What's the score?" he asked, his curiosity undeniable.

She chuckled, her confidence returning in full force. "Given that our Indian squad can turn the game at any point, we shouldn't worry about the score too early. My friend, the game has just begun."

Sameer's laugh followed, warm and genuine. He admired her unshakable assurance, the quiet faith she carried with her even amid uncertainty.

"Hey, I've got a question for you," she said, her tone changing. "Which feeling do you think is the most uncomfortable?"

He paused, his brow furrowing in thought. "No, I've never really thought about it. What about you? What do you think?" he asked, genuinely curious.

She exhaled slowly, the question lingering in the air like an unspoken truth. "Hmm. To me, it's either escaping from the situation or continuing to live with a sense of discomfort. Do you agree?"

"Yeah," he said, nodding slowly. "It does have a profound meaning. I didn't know 'my Kido' thought so deeply."

Her smile softened at the nickname, and they both burst into laughter, the tension between them evaporating for a moment.

After a brief pause, she said, "I'm sure you're wondering why I brought this up. "The only reason I brought it up is so that we may try to accept the discomfort you're now avoiding. Let's not atleast ask the house keeping staff to not enjoy the game."

"Ok. So, what's the plan?" he asked.

"How about we play a game to make the most of this evening? Are you ready?" she asked, her voice cheerful and eager.

"Okay, Ma'am," he replied, the humour in his voice betraying a bit of nervous excitement.

"First, let's sit comfortably on the couch," she instructed as they both settled in, the familiar warmth of their conversation bringing a sense of ease. Once settled, she began to outline the rules of the game.

"Without wasting too much time, we must quickly list the things that made you happy today," she said, her voice clear and direct.

He agreed immediately. “Of course! Ladies first,” he said with a playful wink.

“Why women? Do you think women are weak?” She asked, her tone laced with playful teasing.

“Not at all, no!” he quickly protested. Being unable to bear children rather makes me the weaker gender. Every time I see a pregnant woman, I think, “I wish I could know the feeling.”

She laughed softly, but the humour in her voice carried a hint of surprise.

“By the way, you’re not a lady yet. You’re still sixteen!” he added, a teasing grin spreading across his face.

Kiara burst into laughter at his words, her infectious giggles filling the air. After a brief pause, she regained her breath, wiping away a tear from her eye. “Even though that sounded incredibly cliched, I’ll still consider it a compliment,” she said, grinning broadly.

She gestured for him to begin, and he did, her smile softening as he shared his thoughts. “I’m not joyful. I’m furious. I want to know the result of the game as soon as possible. Everyone today is trying to test my patience. But you,” he said, turning toward her, “you’re the one who makes me smile practically every day. I can at least vouch for that, based on our previous interactions. From the moment you asked me for the newspaper to your comment just now. There’s something about you that makes me smile—maybe it’s those adorable dimples.”

His eyes gleamed with fondness; the memory of their first meeting still fresh in his mind. For a moment, she was taken aback. He had remembered that day—the day she had asked him for the newspaper. Her face reddened, a blend of embarrassment and astonishment. She wasn't used to receiving such praise, and she felt like curling up in a cocoon, hiding her smile behind her hair.

Before she could respond, a loud cheer erupted from the kitchen, catching their attention.

"What happened?" he asked, his eyes wide as he hurried to the kitchen.

Inside, Manoj hugged him, grinning ear to ear. "Maza aagya, sir. Chakka pada!"

He returned to the living room, his grin wide as ever, the tension momentarily forgotten.

"You see, I warned you not to worry too much. Nurture your optimism," said her with a playful glint in her eyes as she leaned back, savouring the moment. "Anyway, I have a gut feeling that India will win the World Cup this year, and that the trophy from the quarterfinals will end up in our possession."

Sameer couldn't help but smile at her words, the easy confidence in her tone both reassuring and a little contagious. She gave him a playful look, her eyes gleaming with both amusement and curiosity.

"Well, if India wins today's game, I'll take you out for ice cream. You would love this new ice cream place."

Her lips curled into a knowing smirk. She'd seen through his attempt to make it sound like a casual offer. It was more of a challenge, a bet wrapped in the guise of a treat. She decided to play along, hiding the excitement that stirred within her.

"Deal," she said, her voice calm but her heart racing a little with the thrill of it all.

He lifted an eyebrow, clearly satisfied with her response. "Excellent! Now, how about a coffee before we head out?"

Her face immediately dropped, her usual calm faltering. "Sorry, but I don't like coffee," she replied, her tone devoid of any remorse. Coffee had never been my thing.

"Not to worry, ma'am! For young babies like you, I do have hot chocolate in my room. Would you like to give it a try?" he suggested, a mischievous smile tugging at the corners of his lips.

"Sure, but I prefer it thick," she replied with a soft chuckle, her eyes narrowing with playful intent.

"Thick? As thick as you like, Ma'am," he replied, bowing dramatically, as though it was some grand gesture. "I'll take care of it."

She laughed, her earlier annoyance melting away in the warmth of the moment. Together, they made their way to his room. The air felt lighter as they walked, their laughter filling the halls like music. Once inside, she straightaway headed to the balcony, the cool wind coming off the lake brushing against her face. She leaned against the handrails, closing her eyes for a moment, as if the world around her had ceased to exist. The soft breeze tugged at her dress, making it billow like it had a life of its own, and a shiver ran up her spine. Her skin prickled with goosebumps, but she remained there, lost in the tranquillity that had settled over her. Meanwhile, Sameer added a few Arabic coffee beans to the machine, setting the stage for the perfect brew. He adjusted the machine's timer with precision, ensuring the milk would boil to the ideal consistency—thick, silky, and smooth—just as she had asked. When he returned to check on her, he stopped in his tracks. She was standing by the balcony, her arms wrapped around herself, rubbing away the goosebumps from the cold. Her smile was peaceful, serene, as if she was in another world entirely. He watched her, his gaze lingering on her profile, his thoughts drifting. He didn't want to interrupt the moment, not yet. Finally, the machine signalled that the brewing cycle had finished, breaking his reverie. He turned back towards the counter, moving slowly, deliberately. He poured his coffee into an exquisite porcelain cup with care, the liquid dark and rich. The hot chocolate, perfectly thick and velvety, filled a tall mug. With a quiet smile, he walked toward her, holding the cup and mug in hand. "Cheers to a good life," he said softly, offering her the steaming mug of hot chocolate.

"Careful, it's thick and hot."

Kiara turned to face him, a soft laugh escaping her lips as she accepted the mug. "Thank you," she said, her eyes meeting his for just a moment. The warmth of the drink seemed to match the warmth in the room, and she felt a small flicker of contentment in the simple exchange. As she took her first sip, the rich taste of the hot chocolate enveloped her senses, and for a fleeting second, all the world outside seemed distant. In that moment, it was just the two of them, sharing a quiet joy in the calm of the evening.

"It's heaven," she murmured, her voice soft but full of appreciation. The flavour was like nothing she had ever tasted before, smooth and indulgent, with a richness akin to melted Belgian truffle. "I had no idea you could make such fantastic hot chocolate," she said, her voice full of surprise and admiration. "This is too good to have just once."

He smiled at her praise, clearly pleased. "Wow. Thank you, Ma'am," he replied, his voice laced with gratitude.

She wrapped her hands around the porcelain mug, holding it for a moment as the warmth seeped into her palms, driving away the chill that still lingered. She let out a satisfied sigh, relishing the peaceful comfort of the moment.

"This place is quite serene, isn't it?" Sameer inquired, his voice softer, as though he, too, was soaking in the calm surroundings. "Now, you won't be able to hear the sounds from the kitchen as well," she added with a knowing smile. They both chuckled softly. The air around them was calm and comforting, the perfect stillness settling over them without the need for many words. The shared silence seemed to speak volumes, their eyes locking as they both understood the quiet connection between them. Breaking the silence, she asked, "Do you listen to music?" Her curiosity seemed to pull them out of the peaceful reverie they were in.

"Yes, I do."

"What kind of music do you like?" she inquired, tilting her head slightly.

"I love ghazals, but I don't have any of my CDs with me right now. Why don't you sing? Do you sing?" he teased.

Her face flushed a little at the thought. "Ghazals are too hi-fi for me! I won't be singing at all," she admitted shyly, trying to hide her discomfort behind a playful tone.

"I enjoy Hindi music. It nourishes my soul, helps me forget my problems, and takes me to a completely different realm. Is it the same for you as well?"

"Well, of course, yes. And if I knew you, you would want to hear precisely romantic Bollywood tunes, right?"

She flashed a wide smile, clearly enjoying the conversation. He smiled, his eyes gleaming with a mischievous spark. After a moment of thought, he pulled up a playlist on his phone, selecting the top 100 love songs from a music app. He paired his phone with a Bluetooth speaker, the soft hum of music filling the space around them. The first song that played was "Yeh Raatein Yeh Mausam," its melody sweet and familiar, the perfect soundtrack to the night they were sharing. Sometimes, all you need is the right song at the right time to make everything feel complete.

"Where words fail, music speaks." – Unknown.

And in that moment, the song seemed to perfectly encapsulate the feelings between them, a gentle harmony of affection, connection, and unspoken gratitude. Kiara's face lit up as she listened, her eyes closing for a moment as she hummed softly along with the tune. "That's indeed a very delightful song! One of my favorites," she said, her voice barely above a whisper. When he saw her smile and heard her hum, he felt a rush of joy. He couldn't help but smile himself, feeling an unspoken understanding pass between them. They were lost in their own thoughts yet lost in each other at the same time. Time seemed to slip by unnoticed. They had completely forgotten about the cricket match until the sound of loud celebrations, cheers, and fireworks signalled that India had won. The streets were alive with the sound of victory, and it brought them both back to reality.

"Oh no! We missed the match! Let's go check the kitchen for the latest news."

Laughing, Kiara followed him to the kitchen. The entire housekeeping staff was busy dancing and celebrating, their joyful noise overwhelming any chance of hearing the match commentary. The atmosphere was electric, and Kiara couldn't help but smile at how infectious the energy was. Being surrounded by such happy, lively people made her feel fortunate, grateful for the moment.

"We should go to your room and watch the highlights," she suggested, the excitement of the victory still lingering in her voice.

"Yeah, we totally forgot! We have a television in there."

Back in his room, he switched on the television, and they watched the highlights. As the award ceremony unfolded and Yuvraj Singh was named Man of the Match,

Sameer let out a small sigh. "I wish I had watched the game live," he said, regret creeping into his voice. She looked at him with a playful smile tucked her lips. "It's time for you to keep the promise you made a while ago," she said, getting up from the couch.

"Which one?" he asked, his brow furrowing. "Did I make any promises to you?"

She clenched her hands together, pretending to be angry. "Shall we go out for ice cream? You've lost to me," she teased.

With a dramatic bow, he stood up from the couch. "Indeed, Ma'am. Without a doubt, I remember this," he said with a grin. She blushed, her heart skipping a beat at the sight of his enticing smile and those gorgeous brown eyes. Trying to contain her emotions, she turned away quickly to change into something more comfortable for their ice cream outing. They decided to go to Arun's, a famous ice cream place nearby. As they headed out, Sameer's phone rang. It was his wife. Kiara, recognizing the situation, quietly urged him to answer. He spoke to his wife and children along the way while a small surge of grief creeping into Kiara's heart. He had been married for six years and had two children. As they made their way to the ice cream shop, he continued his conversation with his family, leaving Kiara to enjoy the quiet moments of their shared journey. He smiled at her understanding and quickly hung up the phone.

"Sorry about that," he said, his tone apologetic. "My kids were being a bit clingy."

She waved it off, her expression relaxed. "You don't have to feel sorry. I understand. Let's order now."

With a nod, he stepped up to the counter and they both began to pick out their favorites. As they exchanged a few playful comments about ice cream choices, the small moment felt warm and comfortable, as though the earlier interruption had never happened. While he was making the payment, one of the staff members handed a marker to Kiara, guiding her towards the cardboard cutouts of the cricket players. She glanced at the cutouts of iconic players like Sachin, Dravid, and Dhoni, each adorned with cheerful messages from other fans.

"Would you like to leave a comment."

"Sure."

Her eyes now scanning the space for a spot to leave her mark. She walked over to Dravid's cutout, feeling a connection to the player, and wrote, "I love you," with a swift, confident stroke. Just as she finished, she looked up to see him walking back with the ice cream cones, his gaze falling on her comment.

"What have you written?" he asked, curious.

"I love you," her eyes meeting his. The moment was suddenly charged with an unexpected tension. The air between them seemed to thicken, and for a moment, Kiara could almost hear her heartbeat in the silence. She shifted uncomfortably, trying to ignore the strange fluttering in her chest. Her gaze wandered, but she could still feel his eyes on her. The ice cream in her hand was starting to melt, but her mind was far away, caught in a swirl of confusion.

Sameer shifted slightly, still unsure whether to respond to the words she just said. His hesitation hung in the air like a question neither of them could voice. He cleared his throat. "You love Dravid, huh?" he asked, his tone casual, yet with a hint of tension, as if he were trying to understand what had just transpired between them. She nodded quickly, forcing a smile, but it felt awkward on her lips. "Yeah, I do," she murmured, almost to herself. Her eyes flicked away, studying the ice cream in her hand, but she couldn't shake the feeling that the words weren't just about Dravid anymore. That voice inside her continued to whisper, you know why. But she wasn't ready to face it yet, wasn't ready to acknowledge the shift that had been brewing between them all along. The moment felt fragile, and she didn't want to break it, but she couldn't shake the unease either. The seconds dragged on, thick with unspoken things. Sameer, sensing the tension, smiled awkwardly. "Well, Dravid is definitely a legend," he said, trying to break the quiet, though his smile didn't quite reach his eyes.

"Let's eat before it melts," he said, gently bringing her back to the present.

She nodded, grateful for the shift in focus. But deep inside, her mind replayed her words—I love you—and she couldn't help but wonder if she had meant them in a way, she wasn't quite ready to admit. As they reached the guesthouse, she couldn't help but feel a sense of comfort in the quietude of the evening. The cool breeze added to the peaceful atmosphere, and the walk had left them both feeling relaxed, albeit a bit sticky from their melting ice cream.

Once inside, Sameer led the way to his room, a casual invitation that felt completely natural between the two of them. "Come on in, make yourself comfortable," he said, gesturing toward the couch as he switched on the TV. She smiled, grateful for the easy camaraderie they shared. She settled onto the couch, smoothing her dress before looking up at him as he fiddled with the remote. "So, highlights again?" she joked, half-smiling, recalling how deeply he had been absorbed in the game earlier.

Sameer chuckled, casting her a quick glance. "What can I say? It's like a reflex," he said with a grin, as the cricket highlights began to play. "I promise we can watch something else afterward, if you like."

For a moment, she nodded, but her attention soon drifted. The highlight reel, filled with replays and expert commentary, wasn't exactly captivating her. She shifted uncomfortably, realizing how much she'd prefer to do something different than watch yet another analysis of the game.

"Hey, I'm kind of losing interest in this… Can we watch something else?" She smiled awkwardly, not wanting to be impolite, but longing for a bit more variety.

"Oh? Why? What's up?" he asked, genuinely curious.

"I think I'm more in the mood for something light-hearted. I've had enough cricket for the night," she admitted.

"Fair enough," he said, then reached for his phone to browse through options. "How about something funny? I've got a comedy film lined up for just this occasion."

"Perfect," she said, relaxing into the couch.

As he queued up the movie, the mood in the room shifted from the intense focus of the cricket highlights to something more carefree. The laughter and light-heartedness of the film began to fill the room, and she found herself sinking into the comfort of the moment BUT it was short lived. Kiara's craving for Panipuri had started out as a spontaneous desire, born more from an underlying feeling of dissatisfaction than actual hunger. But as the time dragged on in Sameer's room, she couldn't help but wonder if it wasn't just the food she was yearning for. The deeper sense of longing, the restlessness she felt, seemed to have been transferred into her craving for that chaotic, spicy street food.

"Hey, I am craving for Panipuri."

Sameer broke into laughter.

"Wow! Panipuri, at this hour, and that too in Chennai!" he exclaimed, clearly amused.

She rolled her eyes playfully, trying to hide the discomfort gnawing at her. "I know it's impossible to find it here at this time, but you won't get it. It's not just about the food," she responded, her voice fading as a sense of longing swept over her.

Her eyes flitted away, unable to keep the vulnerability from creeping in.

Sameer's playful demeanour quickly turned to concern when he noticed the change in her mood. He gripped her shoulders gently and, in a rare serious tone, asked, "Could you wait in my room for a bit? I'll be right back."

"Yes, I'll wait but tell me what's going on in that head of yours," she said, looking at him with curious eyes.

With a wink and a quiet smile, he donned his jacket and left the room, leaving her with a whirlwind of emotions.

Kiara sat on the couch, trying to distract herself, but she was acutely aware of the awkwardness that seemed to permeate the space. She started to read the book he had left behind, but her mind kept wandering back to this craving that seemed to go beyond just food. She couldn't shake the feeling that it was tied to a deeper need - perhaps for connection or attention. As the minutes turned to hours, her thoughts grew heavier, and soon her eyelids grew heavy too. The clock read 1:15 AM when she finally drifted off, her mind full of questions about why she had acted on such a silly whim. The sound of the bell ringing at 2:30 AM jolted her awake. Her heart skipped a beat, and she sprang out of bed, furious. "Where have you been?" she nearly screamed as she opened the door, ready to let loose. But all of that vanished the moment she saw him standing there, holding a bag full of Poori and aloo masala, grinning from ear to ear. Her irritation dissolved into a mixture of surprise and excitement.

Without thinking, she grabbed the bag and raced to his bedside table, her earlier frustration forgotten. She took the Pooris out, filled them with the masala, and squeezed fresh lemon over the top. Despite the lack of the spicy water, she so craved, she took a bite and sighed with pleasure. "This… this is bliss," she exclaimed, the joy of finally getting what she wanted written all over her face. He laughed, clearly pleased with himself. "I may not have gotten the spiced water, but I'm glad you like it. He took a bite too, sharing the experience with her. They ate in silence for a while, exchanging occasional glances and making playful expressions as they stuffed the crispy, spicy Pooris into their mouths. Kiara's stomach ached with happiness, but as she set down her plate, she couldn't help but ask, "You still haven't told me how you managed to get this so late."

Sameer leaned back, a gleam in his eye. "Well, I have a friend, who lives nearby. She works night shifts and gets home around 1:30 AM. I figured I could find some Panipuri there. "Anything for you, sweetheart," he said, the final word filled with both warmth and a touch of mischief. She was taken aback by his thoughtfulness, feeling a warmth spread through her heart. The thoughtfulness behind his gesture, the effort he had gone to, moved her more than she could express. She wasn't sure how to react, but before she could say anything, he leaned closer, placing a gentle hand on her waist, drawing her attention. She froze for a moment, suddenly feeling the heat of his touch and the closeness between them.

She felt the instinct to pull back, but something in her heart whispered, "Let it be." It was like a sudden rush of warmth engulfing her as she allowed herself to stay in the moment. The world around them seemed to disappear as Sameer pulled her into a soft embrace. She felt the warmth of his body, his breath against her ear, and for the first time, something about the closeness felt right. There was no fear or discomfort, just a sense of calm she had never known. She hesitated, her mind racing, unsure of what to do with the emotions bubbling up inside her. But the moment stretched on, and she couldn't quite bring herself to pull away. Breaking the silence, she finally spoke, her voice quiet. "It's late. I should go," she whispered, her pulse still pounding. He gently released her and smiled, though there was something lingering in his gaze. "Okay," he said softly, though his smile never faltered. Kiara walked out of his room, her mind still spinning. There was so much she didn't understand, so many emotions that eluded her comprehension. As the door closed behind her, she wondered what all of this meant. One thing was certain though—the evening had changed something between them, and she wasn't sure what would come next. The walk to her room felt like a slow, aching journey, each step weighed down by the part of her heart she had left behind. It clung to him, yearning for the warmth of his embrace, the solace of his presence. She ached for him in a way that words couldn't capture—desperate to hold him, to whisper the words she feared to say. I love you. But doubt tangled with her courage; she wasn't sure of her own heart, and the possibility of rejection stung like an open wound she wasn't ready to face. Her eyes blurred with the salt of unshed tears as she unlocked the door and stepped inside. The room, bathed in darkness, offered no answers—only the restless thrum of her heartbeat and the silence that swallowed her every thought. She collapsed onto the edge of the bed, staring at the ceiling, eyes wide open, seeking comfort from the chaos in her mind. She tossed and turned, the weight of unspoken words pressing down on her chest. Frustrated, Kiara rose and walked to the balcony, her reflection staring back at her in the glass. "What the hell is happening?" she muttered, but the mirror gave no reply. A faint melody, Kya yehi pyar hai, drifted into her ears, or was it just the echo of her own heart? Love, they said, was a thief of sleep, and tonight, it had stolen hers. Restless, she slid into her plush slippers, running a hand through her tousled hair as she made her way to his room. She knocked lightly; the sound almost lost in the quiet of the night. "Come in, my door is always open for you," he called, his voice like a beacon in the darkness. His response assured her he wasn't asleep either. "I'm having a troubled sleep tonight," she confessed, her voice a soft whisper in the stillness.

"We both are sailing in the same boat," he replied, his words gentle, understanding, as he pulled her closer. "But you didn't know until now. Come here, my sweetheart." His arms encircled her, drawing her in with an ease that made her feel like she was exactly where she was meant to be. The world faded around them as he pressed her against his chest, his heartbeat steady, a rhythm that brought peace to her restless soul. "When you're near me," he whispered, "I feel at ease, calm… all my concerns fade away. Do you feel the same?"

She tilted her head, resting it on his shoulder, her breath mingling with his. "What do you think?" she asked, her voice gentle, carrying the weight of her unspoken emotions. The room seemed to hum with a quiet magic—dim light, soft music, and her laughter like a breeze that filled the space between them. Her heart fluttered, knowing that, in this moment, they were both lost in each other. With a tenderness that spoke of more than words could convey, he kissed her forehead and ran his fingers through her wavy hair, the simple gesture a promise of something deeper. "Shall we try to sleep together?" he asked, his voice laced with affection. She nodded, her heart swelling with something she couldn't quite name, but it felt like home. He gathered her in his arms, the blanket cocooning them both as she rested her head on his chest, seeking comfort in his warmth. The hours stretched on, the world outside forgotten, as she caressed his hair, the motion soothing them both into a peaceful slumber. In his arms, the restless ache of her heart finally quieted, and for the first time in what felt like forever, she found the sweet solace of sleep, tangled in the little pleasures of life, and in the tender embrace of the one she loved. Later, as the night deepened, she rolled towards him, her heart full of longing, and sighed contentedly when she felt the warmth of his presence. She nestled against him, feeling the rise and fall of his chest, the steady rhythm of his breath soothing her restless thoughts. For a fleeting moment, she wished to stay there, wrapped in his embrace, her fingers tracing the outline of his chest, holding him as though the world outside no longer mattered. But as his steady breathing told her he had drifted into sleep, she quietly slipped from his arms, careful not to disturb the peace they had found together. She returned to her own room, the cool air brushing her skin, and turned off the lights. But this time, when she lay down, there was no tossing and turning. Her mind, no longer burdened by uncertainty, began to quiet. In the stillness, she realized that the thoughts of him that had once felt like fragments of a dream were now her waking reality. With her eyes closed, the images of their moments together lingered, their love blooming in the quiet corners of her mind.

As her eyelids fluttered closed, she realized with a soft smile that the dreams of being with him, the soft whispers and quiet touches, had woven themselves into her reality. Dreaming while awake had become a sweeter escape than sleep itself—a beautiful, endless moment suspended in time, where the love she had once only imagined now lived in her heart, alive and true.

"*Love isn't something you find. Love is something that finds you.*"

– *Loretta Young*

Chennai, 2011

Coffee and Crushed Dreams

Kiara woke to the soft, melodic chirping of birds, their song weaving through the stillness of the morning. She felt a surge of energy, yet confusion clouded her thoughts. Was it morning or evening? The passage of time seemed irrelevant; she had drifted to sleep thinking of him, and now, the exact moment of slumber was lost in the haze of her dreams. As she lay on the bed, her messy hair tangled around her pillow, her swollen eyes reflecting the traces of a restless night, she felt the weight of life's unpredictability. Is this how life works for everyone? she wondered, her thoughts a swirl of curiosity. Do other people experience these unexpected twists, the way life surprises you with the most unanticipated moments? Who would have imagined that the little things Sameer did, the small gestures of kindness, would have woven her heart into his so completely? And who could have foreseen that her first love would belong to someone else—a married man with a family, bound to another life, another world?

Lost in the labyrinth of her emotions, she pondered the nature of love, of lies, of the fragile threads that connected them all. It was then that a soft knock at the door interrupted her thoughts. She jumped up, her heart leaping with the hope that it might be him, that he might have woken up, that the distance of the night would be erased with his presence. But as she opened the door, her smile faded. It was one of the guesthouse staff to take her breakfast order. Her face fell, disappointment clouding her features as she mechanically gave her order, the weight of her unmet hopes sinking in. Closing the door softly, she glanced at the clock—8:00 a.m. The numbers seemed cold and distant. She stood for a moment, lost in thought, before stepping outside to the living room, half-expecting to find him there, basking in the early light. But as her eyes scanned the living room, she saw no sign of him, no trace of the warmth they had shared the night before. Her heart sank, and a wave of sadness swept over her. The memory of their closeness, the quiet intimacy, now felt like a distant dream—one that might never fully materialize. The realization left her feeling hollow, as if a part of her had been left behind in the shadows of the previous night. She had hoped, foolishly, perhaps, that the morning would bring clarity, that the empty space between them would be filled. But now, standing alone in the quiet of the garden, she was left to face the painful truth—that some things, no matter how deeply desired, might never be.

"Did I do the right thing?" She murmured, her voice a quiet plea within the stillness of her thoughts. But as always, there was no answer. It was as though her subconscious had withdrawn into its own labyrinth of confusion, leaving her stranded without the clarity she sought. Life, it seemed, was beyond her control. The circumstances had unfolded in ways she could not have anticipated, and all she could do was surrender to them. Brushing aside the tumult of emotions that threatened to overwhelm her, she quickly dressed for work, moving through the motions like an automaton. She left her room without sparing him another thought, or perhaps it was just that the weight of the night before had made her numb. Like every other day, she found herself walking through the lifeless glass-and-steel structure of her office, the familiar faces offering nothing but the usual polite greetings as she passed them by. The elevator doors closed with a soft ding as she stepped inside. Her laptop hummed to life before her as she sifted through emails, trying to focus. She began listing her tasks for the day, but it felt as though the words blurred together, refusing to form any coherent plan. A simple checklist became an ordeal to create, and with each line she wrote, the weight of the previous night pressed harder on her chest. She couldn't focus. It was as though her mind was divided—one part still tethered to him, to the overwhelming emotions she had tried so hard to push away, while the other struggled to stay grounded in the demands of the day. Time and again, she encountered setbacks with her project, and now, it seemed, the same chaos was spilling over into her personal life. Was God punishing her? The thought swirled in her head, an unwelcome whisper that refused to be quieted. She had come to Chennai to prove herself, to establish her worth in a world that seemed to demand more than she could give. But now, she found herself distracted, lost in thoughts of him, her heart and mind pulled in a thousand different directions.

"What's happening to me?" she asked herself, staring blankly at the screen. She had never felt like this before. She was the girl who had always been in control, the one who set goals, made plans, and executed them with precision. Now, she was unravelling, unable to focus on anything for long enough to make any progress. And all of it was because of him. She had never imagined that love could be such a force, one that could disrupt her carefully constructed life and make her forget who she was. Was this really love? she wondered. It felt like her world had been turned upside down in a matter of days, her attention no longer on her goals, her ambitions, but on nurturing something that, for all she knew, might not even last. She couldn't reconcile the person she used to be with the one she had become—a woman distracted, anxious, filled with doubts, unsure of her own path and caught up in a whirlwind of emotions for a man she barely knew. What had happened to the self-esteem, the promises she had made to herself? With a heavy heart and a mind full of mixed emotions, she sat at her desk, trying to summon the focus she so desperately needed. The day wore on, and soon she found herself tangled in a series of minor crises, each one seemingly insignificant on its own but, if left unresolved, capable of leading to disaster.

The time kept on passing, she had completely forgotten about him. Or at least, she thought she had. Amidst the swirling chaos of her thoughts and the relentless buzz of deadlines at work, a soft beep pierced through the cacophony. Her eyes darted to the phone screen, and there it was—a notification from him. A wave of warmth washed over her, despite the storm inside her. She leapt from her chair, her heart skipping a beat, and hurried to the "Refreshment Zone," a quiet corner where she could steal a moment of peace.

With trembling hands, she opened his message: "Hi," followed by a string of smiling emojis. It felt like a small breath of fresh air amidst the overwhelming rush of the day. "Sorry we couldn't meet for breakfast. I was very sleepy. How are you doing?"

A smile tugged at the corners of her lips, but she quickly suppressed it. She had wanted to tell him how much she missed him, how the morning had felt incomplete without his voice, but the weight of her feminine pride held her back. Why should she surrender so easily? What if he took her presence for granted? What if, behind that charming exterior, there lay a side of him she was yet to uncover—someone who would see her vulnerability as a weakness? She typed quickly, almost mechanically, her words colder than she felt: "I'm fine. I was in a hurry today, so completely forgot to see you this morning."

The message sent, her chest tightened, but she quickly dismissed the fluttering doubt that crept into her mind. Yet, almost immediately, his reply came: a string of confused and angry emoticons. The smile he had sent her felt like a distant memory now, replaced by a look she couldn't quite read. He had no idea that beneath her carefully crafted words lay a heart quietly yearning for him, afraid to speak its truth. Her heart began to race, a rhythm she couldn't quite comprehend. It was as though something deep within her was stirring, something fragile and elusive, pulling her in all directions. The bitter-sweet memories of watching her classmates fall in love—those innocent, fleeting moments in school and college—rushed at her like waves crashing relentlessly against a distant shore. The sweetness of their joy mingled with the bitterness of her own reality, leaving her caught in the undertow of longing and loss. Her life had never allowed her the luxury of love, not in the way others had experienced it. The weight of societal expectations and the constraints of her domestic situation had always kept her tethered, her dreams of love nothing more than distant echoes. She had never known the freedom to have someone beside her, someone who could fill the empty spaces with the warmth and happiness she had always craved. Instead, love remained a distant star, its glow dimmed by the circumstances that governed her existence. And yet, despite the harshness of her reality, Bollywood films had always been her escape. They painted a canvas of love so vivid, so pure, that even her soul couldn't help but be marked by it. She had learned about love not from experience, but from the vibrant, idealized tales on the screen—where love was always grand, never messy, always rewarding. It was a paradox of life, a cruel irony: to be surrounded by stories of romance, yet never able to fully touch its warmth. And in that space, she lingered, caught between the dream and the reality, torn between what could be and what was.

As Kiara drifted deeper into the whirlpool of memories, a sudden jolt brought her back to the present. A coffee emoticon flashed on her screen, accompanied by a question mark and a follow-up message: "In the evening?" Her heart fluttered. She could almost feel his presence through those words, the gentle curiosity that made her pulse quicken.

Blushing, she typed back, "What time?"

"At 6:00 p.m., I shall pick you up from the guest house."

Suppressing the smile that was about to appear, she typed, "Okay. See you then." The screen blinked back a confirmation—his response, as simple as it was, felt like a promise.

As she stared at her phone, a rush of emotions washed over her. "OMG! What's happening to me? Am I going bananas over this guy? I've never felt like this before!" she thought, her mind buzzing with the new and intense feeling of desire and excitement. Conversations with him had always made her feel lighter, like the clouds in her sky were parting and letting the sunshine through. But now, it was something more. She was in a happy place, a space where everything seemed to move faster, as if the universe itself was conspiring to bring her joy. The work that had once felt like a mountain now seemed to melt away. In the hours that followed, it was as if time itself had no bearing—her focus was laser-sharp, her fingers dancing across the keyboard, working at twice her usual pace. But, as much as she tried to immerse herself in the rhythm of productivity, a quiet voice in her mind refused to be silenced. It asked questions, whispered doubts. What should I wear? What will we talk about? Why did he ask me out for coffee? These thoughts lingered, slipping through the cracks of her concentration like persistent shadows, impossible to ignore. She smiled to herself in spite of it all, the thought of him filling her with warmth. There was no doubt now—she was caught up in something she couldn't quite understand. It was the first time someone had ever asked her out, and her heart skipped a beat at the significance of it. It was more than just a simple invitation—it felt like an opening, a door to something new. She had to look her best, she decided. After finishing up her work, she managed to leave a little earlier than usual, the thought of meeting him urging her feet forward. By 4:00 p.m., she was already at the guesthouse, her pulse still racing with excitement. She took a quick shower, letting the warm water wash away the tension in her muscles. Wrapping herself in a lemon-yellow bathrobe, she gazed at her reflection in the mirror. She felt as though he were somehow watching her from a distance, his presence lingering even though he wasn't there. She blow-dried her waves, combing them until they shone. She rushed to check the door, she found it bolted, and a strange sense of calm settled over her. "Seems like his absence was becoming equally powerful as his presence," she mused, realizing how profoundly his mere thought had already begun to shape her world. Every second without him felt both impossibly long and wonderfully fleeting. Sweeping aside the whirl of thoughts that had consumed her mind, she walked briskly to her closet, determined to find an outfit that would express the essence of who she was on this pivotal evening. Her fingers brushed against the fabrics, each piece of clothing seeming to mock her indecision. Will this be too revealing? Is this color too dull? Do these stilettoes even match the dress? Her frustration mounted as she tried on one combination after another, each one feeling like it fell short. Dressing up for her first date had suddenly become an impossible task.

The clock ticked relentlessly, and when she glanced up, it was already 5:30 p.m. Panic set in. She had little time left. In a rush, she grabbed one of her favourite pastel-coloured dresses—soft and subtle, just like her personality—and slipped it on. It hugged her figure gently, the color blending perfectly with her skin tone, reflecting the quiet grace she often wished to convey. It was a safe choice, but in that moment, it felt like the right one. She slipped into her heels and, just as she was finishing up, her phone beeped with a new message. "Come outside; will be reaching in 5 mins." Her heart fluttered again. She threw one last glance in the mirror and headed out the door. There, waiting for her at the gate, was him. And to her surprise, he wasn't driving a car, but instead an old, weathered bike that seemed almost as ancient as its rider. She was taken aback as she had expected a sleek, polished vehicle, something that matched the charm of the man before her. But this… this was different. The bike looked uncomfortable, the kind that rattled with every bump in the road. And what unsettled her more was the thought of sitting behind him. She had only known him for two weeks—barely a speck in the timeline of her life—and here she was, about to clutch onto him, a stranger in a very intimate way. Her palms sweated as she took tentative steps toward him. She could feel the burden of her own hesitation. Would he be laughing on the inside at her discomfort? Her body stiffened, and she couldn't help but wonder what he was thinking as he stood there with that confident, almost knowing smile. But there was no turning back now. She eased herself onto the bike, both legs resting awkwardly to one side. She gripped the seat tightly, wishing there was something else to hold on to. The wind in her hair felt strangely vulnerable. She was not sure what was worse: the nerves coursing through her or the uncertainty of what this evening might hold. He seemed to sense her discomfort, adjusting the rearview mirror so he could see her. His smile widened, and there was a warmth in his gaze that made her feel oddly at ease, even if just for a moment. For a split second, everything froze—the anticipation, the awkwardness, the fluttering heartbeat—and in that brief pause, she realized: this was real. A first date. And it had already begun, not in the comfort of predictability, but in the vulnerability of the unknown.

"Shall we go?" he asked, his voice breaking through the anxious fog surrounding Kiara.

"Yes," She responded, her heart racing as the words left her lips.

The ride was smoother than she expected—no jarring bumps or heavy traffic to distract her. The engine hummed beneath them, a soft background to the quiet tension building in her mind. What she hadn't noticed at first was how often he was glancing at her through the rearview mirror. She felt a rush of shyness creeping up her neck as she realized it. Without thinking, she instinctively hid her face behind his back, her hands clutching the sides of the bike to steady herself. She had no intention of giving him that easy gratification, at least not yet. They arrived at Café Coffee Day; a place as familiar as it was cliché. The sign caught her eye as they parked: "A lot can happen over coffee." A small laugh bubbled up in her mind. Seems like no other beverage inspires more chance encounters and first dates than this humble brew, she thought, amused by the irony of it all.

He turned to her, still glancing at her through the rearview mirror. "You can go inside and find a place for us. I'll park the bike and come."

She nodded, a little too quickly, as if eager to step away from the awkwardness of the moment. She took a few tentative steps toward the entrance, her thoughts swirling like the soft breeze that ruffled her hair. Why did he bring me here? she wondered. How do people have intimate conversations at an open café like this, with strangers all around? Another wave of hesitation hit her. Rolling her eyes at herself and suppressing a smirk, she couldn't help but marvel at the bizarre situation. Not being a coffee person, yet here I am, on a coffee date with a man, she mused with a shake of her head. The dichotomy of life! Love truly changes your preferences... and your priorities, she murmured to herself, half in disbelief. Perhaps it was the magic of the moment, or it was just the pull of something new, but she knew one thing for certain: she was already transforming, in ways she never expected.

Kiara didn't notice him walking towards her after parking the bike. She was so lost in her thoughts, consumed by the swirling emotions of the day, that she barely registered his presence until he tapped her lightly on her shoulders.

"Can we go inside? I thought you would have already found a table for us!" he said, his voice full of playfulness.

Kiara blinked, startled, as her thoughts returned to the moment. "Oops! Sorry, I was just lost," she apologized, a shy smile spreading across her face.

He extended his hand to her, his smile warm and reassuring. "That's okay, let's go now."

As they entered the coffee shop, the first thing that hit them was the stark contrast in temperature. The warm air outside gave way to the biting cold of the air conditioners inside. Kiara shivered, pulling her jacket closer around her. He noticed and led her to a corner seat, slightly away from the vent, in a cozy, not-so-crowded part of the café. The ambiance of the place was calming. The coffee shop shared its space with a clubhouse, and beyond the glass windows, a swimming pool glimmered in the fading light of the evening. As dusk settled, the soft lighting inside and the tranquil music playing in the background created a soothing, almost dreamlike atmosphere. She couldn't help but feel a sense of peace, despite the whirlwind of thoughts still churning inside her. The waiter soon arrived with the menu. Without even glancing at it, Sameer placed his order with confidence. "I'll have a latte with fresh crème," he said, turning to Kiara. "What would you like?"

Kiara hesitated, her eyes scanning the menu but finding it all a bit overwhelming.

"I'm going to take some time to decide. I hope you don't mind?"

"Nope, that's fine!" he replied with a smile that eased some of her tension.

Flipping through the pages of the menu, she tried to fill the silence with conversation.

"It seems like you love coffee and come here often!" she remarked, noticing the ease with which he ordered.

His smile widened.

"Yes, very much. Coffee keeps me going until it's time for wine." His tone was light, playful, and she couldn't help but laugh.

Seeing the confusion still lingering in her eyes, he leaned forward, trying to be helpful. "Do you know what goes best with a cup of coffee?"

Kiara raised an eyebrow. "What?"

"Another cup," he said with a grin.

She smiled at his answer, rolling her eyes in mock exasperation. "I'm not too keen, but if you say so," she replied, finally giving in to the moment. With a smile, he gestured to the waiter. "Two Café Lattes, please."

As soon as the order was placed, he noticed a change in her. The confusion that had clouded her expression melted away, replaced by a quick flash of relief in her eyes. Perhaps it was the simplicity of the choice, or perhaps it was the way he made her feel more at ease.

"Have you ever visited CCD before?"

"No," she answered, the honesty of her response surprising even her.

It was a small revelation amidst their casual conversation, but one that carried with it a quiet weight. It was the beginning of something she couldn't quite put into words yet. She immediately regretted her words, her mind racing with insecurities. Would he judge me? she wondered. Would he think I'm not 'cool,' that I'm just some outdated girl with no taste, or worse—someone with a terrible, unsophisticated palette? The worry gnawed at her, but she pushed it aside. In that moment, she decided to be honest. She would say it as it was, without hiding behind any pretences. No games, she thought. Just the truth.

"It's my first time here, and first time with you too!"

"I'm honoured," his voice laced with a touch of humour that made her heart flutter.

"You're looking very pretty in this dress."

Kiara's cheeks immediately flushed crimson. "Thank you," she murmured, trying to hide her blush behind her hand, though she knew it was hopeless.

But Sameer's gaze didn't let up. It felt as if his eyes were locking onto hers, intense and searching. She could feel the heat of his stare, and it sent an electric shiver all the way down to her toes, making her uncomfortably aware of how close they were. His expression held something deeper than admiration—something that sent her pulse racing. The way he looked at her made her feel both seen and exposed at once. His smile was warm, inviting, and it lit up his face, making him seem almost otherworldly, like the sun breaking through clouds on a stormy day. His presence radiated a quiet confidence and warmth that made her feel as though everything around them—every little detail—was meant to be. The romantic instrumental music playing in the background, the soft glow of the ambient lighting, the plush dual-toned sofas around them, and the couples on other tables enjoying their own moments of quiet bliss, all created the perfect atmosphere for a date night. Yet, amid all this, they both found themselves at a loss for words.

The silence lingered between them, thick and comfortable, yet charged with something unspoken. Neither of them seemed to know what to say next, both unsure how to bridge the distance between the shy smiles and the fluttering hearts. The rhythm of the evening had shifted, and now, it seemed that both were caught in the delicate dance of trying to say something meaningful, but unsure of where to start. He regarded her thoughtfully, his eyes searching her face as if trying to find the right words to express what had been stirring inside him since they first met. The silence between them was charged, heavy with the weight of unspoken thoughts. Kiara, meanwhile, was desperately hoping for the coffee to arrive soon to break the tension. She feigned a casual glance toward the counter, muttering under her breath, "They are so slow," though her mind was racing with anticipation. After what felt like an eternity, the coffee finally arrived. The cups were carefully prepared, with two delicate hearts drawn in the foam—sweet, simple, yet perfect. She couldn't help but smile at the charming presentation, and before she could say anything, they both laughed in the same breath, stealing shy glances at each other.

Sameer, sensing the moment, stood up and moved from the chair opposite her to the couch where she was sitting. Her heart fluttered, her pulse quickening at the proximity. He settled beside her, his presence overwhelming in the best way, and before she could even process it, he wrapped his arms around her. The gesture was firm, protective, yet there was a tenderness to it that made her feel both comforted and slightly nervous.

"I want to tell you something," he murmured, his voice low and steady, his breath warm against her ear.

Kiara's heart skipped a beat. Her mind spun in circles as she tried to make sense of his words and his touch. A dilemma surged through her chest. She wasn't sure how to react—his embrace was powerful, almost possessive, yet it held a gentle assurance that made her feel both safe and uncertain. Her instinct was to lean in, but fear tugged at her. What if he's just being kind? she wondered. What if he doesn't feel the same way I do? As she tried to steady her breathing, she could feel her pulse thumping in her ears, her hands trembling ever so slightly. She looked up at him, meeting his gaze, and in that moment, she saw something in his eyes—a depth of emotion that left her speechless. Trying to decipher the emotions swirling there, Sameer's words cut through the silence like a sudden chill. "I know I should have told you this yesterday, but I couldn't. I wanted to just be in the moment and not think of anything else," he paused, his gaze intensifying, "I must go home tonight; I won't be back until next week."

Gosh. What the hell? What was she even thinking? And what had he just said? The excitement that had been building up—the first date, the connection, the moments they shared—came crashing down, like an unexpected wave. It was an anti-climax. A gut-punch. First dates never fail to be interesting, but rarely do they leave you feeling this confused. They often make you speechless and, at times, even lost in translation. Kiara's heart sank as his words hung in the air, and she struggled to keep the sting of disappointment from overflowing. Her breath hitched, but she managed to hold back the tears, taking a deep, shaky breath. All she could muster was a soft, defeated, "Okay."

The moment shattered her, leaving her sitting there, trying to gather the pieces of her emotions. Her mind spun as she tried to make sense of it all. Sameer, noticing her turmoil, took a sip from his coffee. Raising his eyebrows slightly, almost as if asking for confirmation. "Okay?" he asked again, uncertain about how to move forward. The silence between them stretched, thick and heavy, as they both sipped their coffee. Kiara's eyes didn't leave his face, but the earlier warmth in the atmosphere had dissipated. The smile still lingered on their lips, but it no longer held the same spark. The euphoria she had felt moments before—those butterflies, that rush—had slowly drained from her, replaced by an overwhelming sense of loneliness, even with him sitting right beside her. She tried to process what he had just told her, trying to reconcile the connection she felt in the moment with the sudden absence he had mentioned. There was no excitement left, no thrill—just a hollow ache settling in her chest. On the other hand, Sameer sat there, watching her closely. He could sense the shift in her energy, the way her demeanour had changed so suddenly. He wanted to say something, anything, to bridge the gap, to somehow ease the discomfort he had unknowingly caused. But neither of them knew what to say. The words felt stuck in their throats. After a few moments of awkward silence, Sameer cleared his throat and tried to lighten the mood. "The coffee is really good," he said, almost a little too casually. "Did you like it?" he asked, taking another sip of his own coffee, hoping to restart the conversation.

Kiara, still lost in her thoughts, blinked and glanced down at her cup. Her mind was in a whirlwind, but she managed a small nod. "Yeah, it's good," she murmured, though her words felt distant and empty, a far cry from the enthusiasm she had felt when they first sat down. The space between them had widened, despite how close they physically were. The feeling of being there, of being present, had faded, leaving only two people trying to find their footing in a conversation that had suddenly become far more complicated than either of them anticipated. She continued to stare at her cup, her smile thin and forced, the words of the world around her muted. Each sip of coffee seemed to grow colder, as did her heart. Somewhere deep inside, Kiara knew that Sameer was fully aware of the shift in her feelings. That was why he had chosen this moment, this place, to tell her he would be leaving. It felt like a carefully calculated goodbye, wrapped in a casual conversation over coffee.

Clearing her throat, trying to mask the pain creeping into her voice, she asked, "Ahem, when is your flight?"

"10:00 p.m. tonight," he replied, his voice steady, almost resigned. "So, we need to leave here soon. After I drop you, I'll return the bike to my colleague, and then head to the airport."

To soften the blow, he added with a light chuckle, "I booked the last flight for today so we could spend some time together, and I don't want to miss it."

Kiara forced a smile, but inside, her heart was sinking. She wanted to feel happy for him, for his ambitions, for his life moving forward—but all she could feel was the emptiness of his absence. She tried to joke, but it came out more desperate than she intended. "I want you to miss your flight," she said. "I want you to knock on my door every night for dinner and every morning for breakfast."

Their eyes met, both searching for something in each other, but neither able to find the right words. In that silence, their hands found each other, their fingers brushing softly before locking together.

"I'll miss your company," he said, his voice quieter now, as though the weight of the words was pressing down on him as much as it was on her. Kiara's heart ached, but she quickly pulled her hand away. Standing up, she forced herself to act composed. "By the time you come back, I might be leaving… or I would have left, if everything goes according to the schedule I've submitted for work." Her words felt hollow, like the finality of a goodbye hanging in the air. Without saying anything, he stood up and walked to the counter to settle the bill. She followed him, her mind a whirlwind of conflicting emotions. As they passed through the café, weaving between tables of laughing couples, animated groups of friends, and families gathered, she couldn't help but feel the weight of the tagline that had greeted them when they first entered: "A lot can actually happen over coffee."

She glanced around the room, and it dawned on her—this café had witnessed countless moments, both joyful and painful. It had been the backdrop to proposals, breakups, new beginnings, and endings. A silent witness to the ebb and flow of life, of love and loss. For her, it was a place of bittersweet memories now—a spot where she'd shared her first moments with Sameer and where she would now, unintentionally, mark the beginning of something uncertain and painful. Her life had been turned upside down in the blink of an eye, and she wasn't sure if it was for better or for worse. Only time will tell, she thought, trying to comfort herself in the face of the unknown. The self-realization hit her like a sudden wave—she had fallen in love with a married man. And now, the fear of losing him before she'd even fully had him was almost too much to bear.

As the saying goes, "As your feelings for someone grow stronger, so does your fear of losing them." Kiara could feel that fear growing inside her, like an undeniable truth she could not escape.

Chennai, 2011

(Un)conditional Love

As Sameer went to fetch the bike, she fought hard to hold back the tears that threatened to spill over. Climbing onto the bike, she gripped his shoulder tightly, her mind racing with the thought that this might be their last ride together. The weight of the unspoken words hung heavy in the air, each second feeling like a fleeting moment of togetherness that she knew would soon slip away. As they sped down the road, the tears that she had desperately tried to hold in began to fall, blurring her vision, as if the world itself was mourning the impending separation. She was thankful that he didn't notice that he was too focused on the road ahead, unaware of the storm brewing inside her. Quickly, she wiped her tears away, pretending that nothing had happened, her heart aching with each passing mile. He glanced into the rear-view mirror and smiled, but his expression faltered as he saw the signs of something more, something hidden deep within her. She clung to him in silence, her emotions too heavy to articulate, and let the wind carry away the tears that continued to fall, hoping they would disappear without a trace. The ride was uneventful, yet every moment felt like an eternity, as if time itself was stretching out, reluctant to let go of their shared moments.

When they reached the guesthouse, the silence between them deepened. He went to his room to pack, and she stood still, watching him with a gaze that seemed empty, as though her very soul had vacated her body. She didn't blink, didn't move—just stared at him with a hollow expression, as if he were already gone. As he finished packing, he turned to her, his face filled with a mixture of concern and affection. He pulled her into a hug, holding her tightly as if trying to freeze time in that one moment. "Wait for me," he said softly, "and don't leave for Gurgaon till I return."

Her heart skipped a beat at his words, her mind going blank, a thousand thoughts colliding with no room to settle. His voice echoed in her mind, but the promise he asked for seemed impossible, and yet she knew, deep down, that she was already waiting—waiting for something that might never come. "Promise me that you won't be leaving," he whispered, his voice barely audible, as if he were afraid to say the words out loud. The question lingered in the air, unanswered, as both stood on the precipice of an uncertain future. Kiara knew that her project would wrap up in just a few days, and that once it did, she would have no choice but to return to Gurgaon. The thought lingered, offering a flicker of hope, yet she knew deep down that the clock was ticking. There was no escaping her obligations, no way to delay the inevitable.

After Sameer left for the airport, she slowly made her way back to her room. Every step felt like a weight added to her already burdened heart. She had been holding herself together for so long, but the moment she stepped inside, she could no longer keep her composure. Emotionally drained, she slumped onto the bed, her body giving in to the exhaustion she had pushed aside for so long. Tears came unbidden, flowing freely as she cried for what she was losing, for what was slipping through her fingers. She felt a hollowness inside, an emptiness that seemed to swallow her whole. The room felt suffocating, and no matter how hard she tried, she couldn't escape the overwhelming sadness. As time passed, Kiara knew it was already time for dinner. Housekeeping had called earlier, reminding her to place an order, but she couldn't find the strength to respond. The thought of eating felt foreign, unnecessary, as if food couldn't fill the void that had settled deep within her. She wanted nothing more than to be alone in her thoughts, to process the swirling emotions that had overtaken her. In that quiet, solitary moment, Kiara's world seemed to shrink down to just one person—Sameer. The love, the longing, the unspoken words, all seemed to concentrate on him. He was all she could think of. And yet, the painful truth was that no matter how much she wished for things to be different, the distance between them was growing with each passing moment. The reality of their love was becoming too clear to ignore. She knew that the future was uncertain, and in her heart, she feared it would never be the same again.

She just wanted to be with him. Her heart ached for him, a deep, insatiable craving that seemed to consume her every thought. After what felt like an eternity of crying, she glanced at the clock, shocked to find that more than two hours had passed. No wonder she felt like she was suffocating, her breaths shallow and quick. Needing some relief, she opened the door to the balcony and cracked her room door slightly, hoping the fresh air would help. She turned up the fan, hoping it would cool her burning skin, and switched on the TV, desperate for any distraction. But of course, the universe had other plans. The music channel on the TV was playing a string of heartbreak songs. Each one seemed to echo her pain, as if the universe was mocking her. It was like a scene from a movie, where the songs you never thought would mean anything suddenly cut through you like a blade. She realized she didn't need to watch reruns of sad movies or TV shows anymore to feel this pain. The heartbreak was already woven into her reality.

Wiping her eyes, she glanced at the clock again, wondering if he had taken off yet. She grabbed her phone, her finger hovering over his number. The thought of him hearing her voice, knowing she was on the verge of falling apart, made her pause. She tossed the phone aside, retreating into her pillow. She couldn't just spill her heart to him so easily, not after everything that has happened. He had come into her life like a burst of light, painting everything in vibrant colours, and then, just as quickly, he was gone, leaving her in the darkness once more. She cursed herself for ever letting her guard down. The noise from the common area outside her room grated on her already fragile nerves. Irritated and overwhelmed, she slammed the door shut, seeking solitude. She moved to the balcony, sitting on the railing, her legs dangling as she stared up at the sky, hoping for some answer. Why was her heart always so full of grief? Her sobs gradually quieted, the tears slowing, and with a deep sigh, she buried her face in her palms, trying to find some comfort in the silence.

"He was never mine. I need to control myself." She repeated the words, as if they were a mantra to calm her racing thoughts. "There are things we never want to let go off, people we never want to leave behind. But letting go isn't the end of the world. It's the beginning of a new life. Isn't it?" She tried to find solace in her own words, the thought of moving forward both comforting and terrifying. Getting down from the railing, she walked to the bedside table, drinking water to soothe her dry throat. Trying to distract herself, she picked up a book and began flipping through its pages, but the words blurred in front of her eyes. Her mind was too tangled with emotions to focus.

A knock at the door interrupted her thoughts. She was too exhausted to care, too drained to feel irritated by the intrusion. She ignored it, her eyes still fixed on the book, trying to drown out the world. But the knocking continued, persistent and unrelenting. Finally, after several moments of hesitation, she dragged herself out of bed and walked to the door. She opened it, and her heart stopped. Standing there, before her, was the last person she expected to see. For a moment, she wasn't sure if she was dreaming or wide awake. A strange mix of emotions—anxiety, relief, relaxation, and happiness—flooded her, but she couldn't find the words to express any of it. Her face remained blank, the whirlwind inside her too powerful to articulate. The silence in the room was so profound that the ticking of the wall clock seemed unnaturally loud. Neither of them spoke, both caught in the intensity of the moment. Then, it hit her—she had been staring at him for far too long, completely lost in the reality of his presence. Without thinking, she threw herself into his arms, her sobs escaping uncontrollably as she clung to him, desperate for the comfort he offered. He held her tightly, his grip steady and reassuring. Gently, he lifted her in his arms and laid her on the bed, his touch soft yet firm.

With a shaky breath, she managed to speak, her voice thick with emotion. "What the hell happened?" Her words were barely a whisper, and her throat was too tight for her to say anything clearly. Sameer, however, didn't seem to try to understand her question. Instead, he simply watched her, worry visible on his face. Her eyes were barely open, and her hair was a tangled mess from the tears. In that moment, all he wanted was to comfort her, to ease the pain he could see in her. He gently pushed the errant strands of hair away from her damp face and, his voice tender, asked, "What's wrong, baby? Why are you crying? Your swollen eyes, your choked throat—it's freaking me out." She didn't answer. She was already drowning in an ocean of emotions, too overwhelmed to find the words to explain herself. She tried to swim toward them, but the words just wouldn't come. He gently wiped away her tears, then cradled her face in his hands, his eyes fixed on hers. His smile never faltered, remaining steady and reassuring. The atmosphere between them was thick with emotions, and no words seemed needed. Some things, he knew, couldn't be described in language—they had to be felt, understood without speaking. He pulled her into his arms again, the warmth of his embrace enveloping her, his energy so powerful it seemed to melt the pain from her heart. The passion, the comfort, the sheer positivity of his presence soothed her soul in a way nothing else could. She leaned her head against his strong arms, feeling the steady beat of his heart beneath her. The bond between them, though new, felt profound—how could he understand her so well? They hadn't shared the same school, college, or workplace, and they weren't even friends before this. They had met just two weeks ago, yet in that short time, he had managed to read her, comfort her, and make her feel alive again. It left her wondering if she held a special place in his heart. His return had brought her comfort, though she couldn't fully explain why. She looked at him as he stepped back briefly to go to the kitchen, noting how little had changed about him. His hair was still messy, his white shirt slightly wrinkled, but there was a touch of worry in his eyes that made him seem all the more real. His energy was infectious, and despite everything, she felt a flicker of warmth in her chest.

In the kitchen, Sameer grabbed a glass of water and placed an order for food, his movements calm and steady. Meanwhile, in the hallway, Manoj, who had been observing from afar, picked up on the change in the air. The unmistakable "love fever" was in the air, and he couldn't help but ask, "Is ma'am, okay?"

Sameer smiled, his voice soft but confident as he replied, "Yeah, she's fine."

After placing the food order, he returned to the room, moving silently as if the air itself was charged with a thousand unspoken words. He sat next to her on one side of the bed, which was cushioned with pillows, and wrapped her gently in his arms. She lifted her face to meet his gaze, her eyes filled with a mix of wonder and uncertainty.

"How come you're here?" she asked softly. "At this time, you were supposed to be on the flight."

He smirked, a mischievous glint in his eyes. "Wow, you realized it too soon!" he teased, making her to smile, though it was shadowed by sadness. He pulled her closer, his arms wrapping around her as he held her hands gently in his. "When I went inside the airport," he began, his voice softer now, "I felt like something wasn't right. It felt like I was leaving something behind. Though I was going to see my kids and my wife after two weeks, strangely, I wasn't excited at all. I stayed in front of the check-in counter for almost half an hour, but I couldn't manage to check in. Something was stopping me."

Kiara's breath caught in her throat, her heart pounding as she waited for him to continue.

"It was you," he said, his voice low but steady. "From the very beginning, it was different with you. I tried to keep my distance, tried not to get too close, but before I realized it, I'd already fallen in love with you. And you know what they say, 'Distance makes the heart grow fonder.', I've always believed that when you love someone, you shouldn't hold back. You should tell them right away, because you never know if life will give you a second chance. So, I missed my flight. I missed it because I wanted to be with you. I needed to tell you how much I love you."

Kiara's heart raced, and she took a shaky breath as she lowered her head, her gaze lingering on their hands. His fingers were wrapped around hers with such tenderness, and the touch sent a ripple of warmth through her body. She could barely find the words to respond.

"You do?" She asked softly, her voice shaking with emotion.

"Yes," said Sameer. His eyes never leaving hers, filled with certainty. "I do. That's why I came back. I couldn't leave without telling you."

Kiara's brow furrowed slightly, a mixture of disbelief and confusion still clouding her mind. "But… how? You hardly know me," she whispered. "I always thought that two people have to know each other well before they fall in love."

Sameer's smile softened; his gaze full of affection. He stroked the back of her hand gently. "I do know you well enough," he replied, his voice unwavering. "The more I learn about you, the deeper I fall in love with you. And right now, I know that I can't imagine my life without you in it."

Her chest tightened, the realization of his words slowly sinking in. She was still trying to make sense of everything—the unexpected depth of his feelings for her, the rush of emotions that seemed to surge between them. But in that moment, as she rested her head against his chest, Kiara knew that nothing else mattered. She didn't need to understand it all—she just needed to let herself feel. And for the first time in a long time, she allowed herself to believe in something real. Her gaze lingered on him as she traced the contours of his face, her eyes traveling from his messy hair to his strong jawline, eventually getting lost in the depth of his eyes. The world seemed to melt away, and for a brief moment, it was just the two of them, suspended in time. His nose brushed gently against hers, and then his hands cupped her face, his fingers sliding to the delicate curve of her neck. His lips, warm and tender, kissed her forehead, her eyes, her cheeks, and then finally found her lips. Each kiss was a promise, a delicate reassurance that left her heart racing and her breath shallow. She gripped his arms, overwhelmed by an unfamiliar sensation of longing and desire that took hold of her. Her body trembled, and she kissed him back, letting herself surrender to the moment. With a soft sigh, he leaned his forehead against hers, pulling her closer into his embrace. She nestled into him, eyes still closed, basking in the comfort of his arms, wishing he would keep holding her, keep kissing her, never letting go. Yet, deep within her heart, a quiet awareness tugged at her. She knew this connection, as beautiful and intense as it was, wouldn't be easy for either of them to navigate.

Mature enough to understand the complexities of their situation, Kiara knew that Sameer was married, with two children. She also knew that if anyone found out about their relationship, it would bring untold consequences, most likely leaving her to face societal stigma and judgment. The reality of their circumstances hovered like a cloud in her mind, but for now, she decided to push those thoughts aside. She wanted to live in this moment with him, to enjoy the growing intimacy between them. She had felt alone for as long as she could remember, disconnected from the world around her. But with him, everything felt different—exciting, new, and thrilling. Yet, there was a touch of fear as well, as she wasn't sure where this would lead or what it might cost her. Still, she allowed herself to revel in the comfort of his arms, the sound of his heartbeat, and the gentle rhythm of their shared silence. They stayed like that for what seemed like an eternity, wrapped in each other's warmth. The quiet was finally broken by a knock at the door, followed by the unmistakable voice of Manoj. He entered carrying a large tray of food, his cheerful face bringing a sudden lightness to the atmosphere. "Sir, pyar badhta hai ek plate mein khane se!!" he declared, his grin barely contained. Kiara and Sameer exchanged amused looks before both breaking into smiles. The moment, so tender and intimate just a second ago, had been lightened by Manoj's playful comment. He handed the tray to Sameer and winked before leaving, his grin lingering as he closed the door behind him. The surprise, though innocent, had brought a burst of joy to the room. Manoj, in his youthful exuberance, had unknowingly captured the warmth and affection that now flowed between Sameer and Kiara. Despite thinking he might not fully understand their bond, his light-hearted intrusion had brightened the moment, reminding them both that sometimes, love can be shared in the most unexpected ways.

Sameer smiled softly; his eyes gleaming with affection. "He's very observant! I didn't expect him to notice what's brewing."

Laughing quietly, he added, "he looks innocent, but he's not!"

As he spoke, he carefully placed the tray on one of the side tables, then poured water into a glass, all while spreading out the newspaper on the bed. He moved the cushions aside to make space for himself and settled next to her. He gestured for her to start eating.

"I'm not hungry. This surprise of yours has quenched my thirst and dissolved my hunger," she replied with a soft smile, her heart full of the intimacy of the moment.

"Baby, you can't live on love and thin air. You need food!" he teased, making her smile again.

But as she reached for the spoon, her face twisted in pain, and the spoon clattered to the tray. Sameer's eyes shot to her hand, noticing the swelling for the first time. "Oh my God! How come I haven't noticed this till now? How did it happen? When I left for the airport, you were fine," he exclaimed, gently taking her hand between his palms, trying to soothe it. The red and blue discoloration was now more visible, a stark contrast to her usual complexion. Without wasting another moment, he rushed out of the room. Manoj, who had been nearby, noticed Sameer's urgency. "Sir, sab theek hai na?" he asked, his tone filled with concern. He didn't respond, his mind solely focused on getting the ice to ease Kiara's pain. He returned swiftly, the ice in hand, and shut the door behind him to ensure privacy. He knelt beside her; his touch gentle as he carefully applied the ice to her swollen hand. The coolness of the ice helped, but it was the tenderness in his touch and the worry in his eyes that soothed her heart.

His concern was palpable as he looked at her, his voice soft but firm. "Promise me! You will see a doctor tomorrow if the pain doesn't subside."

"I will," she whispered, her eyes meeting his, feeling the warmth of his love and care seep into her very soul.

Being near to him bought all her emotions bubbling up to the surface. After a long time, she felt happy as she has finally found someone who cares about her wellbeing; someone who is genuinely concerned about her injury. With flaring nostrils and lips pressed together, he asked, "how did it happen?"

"When I entered the room, I felt empty, empty in my heart and in my stomach. I felt alone. I felt as if I had lost the closest person on earth and in anger, I just punched the wall."

Clasping her hands, he looked into her soulful innocent eyes and spoke with an earnestness in his voice "I'll never leave you alone."

"Wherever you go, whatever you do, I'll be right here waiting for you," he sang the famous Richard Max song.

These words weren't depthless and hence, made her fall for him again and again, every time, more than the last time. Giving her a bear hug, he said, "Baby! I've something to tell you."

Keeping her eyes closed, she asked, "What it is? I'm listening."

"I came today to be with you, to tell you that how much I love you, however I'll have to leave tomorrow. Will you be fine?"

With a pause, she uttered an unconvincing, "yes."

Though she knew that she will not be 'fine' without him being around but there was a hope that they'll be going to see each other again in a week's time.

"Thanks baby. Now, let's have dinner. What would you like to do after we finish our dinner? Would you like to go for a walk or rather watch TV?"

"I want to get some sleep."

"Wait, I'll get a painkiller for you to sleep well."

"No, no, I don't need that."

Completely ignoring her, he pushed a pill between her lips and said, "Fast, chug some water."

He looked at her with a soft smile, though he could see the uncertainty in her eyes. He knew that leaving was going to hurt both, but he had to do it. His family awaited him, and he couldn't ignore that responsibility. Still, the thought of being away from her for even a short time filled him with a sense of unease. He gently swept a loose strand of hair from her face. "I know this won't be easy for either of us," he said softly, his voice calm and comforting. "But I promise, we'll find a way to make this work. I'll come back, and we'll see each other again."

Kiara leaned into him, allowing his warmth to envelop her. She wanted to believe him, wanted to believe that everything could work out despite the complexities of their lives. But the reality of their situation—the fact that he was married and had children—was always at the back of her mind, gnawing at her, making her question whether they could ever truly have a future together.

"I don't want you to go. Can't you be here with me, always."

Sameer's heart ached at her words, but he knew he had to be strong. "I'll always be with you, in every way that I can," he said, pulling her into a tight hug. "You're in my heart, Kiara. And no matter the distance, that will never change." Her head rested on his shoulder, her breath steadying as she found comfort in his presence. Though there were still uncertainties ahead, in that moment, all that mattered was that they were together, and that they had the chance to love each other—if only for a little while longer. He ran his fingers through her hair, planting a kiss on the top of her head. "Let's cherish this time, alright?" We'll create memories that we can hold onto until we see each other again." She nodded, her eyes shut as she absorbed his words, his touch, and the warmth of his love. She wasn't sure what the future held, but she knew that for now, this was enough. If you have seen a frozen bird coming back to life, you would understand exactly what was happening to her life again! With him she had found the elixir of life!

Though Manoj kept Sameer's room ready but that night he didn't go to his room. He slept beside her. She felt needed, important, and most importantly loved!

Next morning, as the sun's warm rays filtered through the balcony, casting a soft glow on the space around them. The peaceful morning seemed to embrace them in a cocoon of comfort. She felt a sense of calm that she hadn't experienced in a long time, as if the world had paused just for them. The playful banter and shared silence between bites of food was a moment she cherished deeply. She looked at Sameer, his usual intensity softened by the morning light. He was enjoying his morning tea and newspaper, but his eyes occasionally shifted toward her with a look of admiration, something she hadn't been used to seeing so openly before. For the first time, she felt truly seen—not just as someone to be cared for but as someone whose presence mattered deeply to him.

"Why didn't you wake me up?"

"I should have but I wanted you to rest well. Come here, Give me a hug. You know, I think this is the happiest I've been in a long time."

She smiled softly, looking into his eyes. "I feel the same way," she replied, her voice carrying the weight of unspoken emotions. "It's nice, being with you like this. It feels real."

"I want to make more moments like this," he said, leaning slightly closer to her. "I know we have a lot to figure out, but I want to spend time with you. Make memories. No matter the challenges ahead."

She felt a warmth spread through her chest, not just from the sun but from the sincerity in his words.

"I have ordered the breakfast already. You go get ready and then we will have it together."

Kiara smiled counting her blessings.

As they enjoy breakfast in a comfortable silence in each other's company, knowing that the future would bring its own set of challenges, but for that moment, they were content in each other's presence. The outside world felt distant and irrelevant, as if the only thing that mattered was the time they were sharing in that small, quiet corner of the world. After a quiet breakfast, the aroma of freshly brewed coffee still lingering in the air, he stood up from the table, his eyes filled with a sense of purpose. He glanced at her, around the room for a moment, taking in the soft glow of the morning sun spilling through the windows. With a gentle smile, he turned toward the door, his mind already on the journey ahead. He had made a promise, one he fully intended to fulfil. "I'll be back soon," he whispered to her.

Stepping outside, the cool morning breeze ruffled his hair, and with that, he set off towards the airport. There was a family, a wife, his children waiting for him, but the promise of coming back soon hung in the air like a tether, pulling him back to everything that mattered most. It wasn't just a promise - it was a vow, a bond, and he was determined to honour it.

> "*Promises are the language of hope, but their fulfilment is the language of love.*"
>
> – *Unknown*

Chennai, 2011

The Miles and the Milestones

Nearly three hours had passed when Kiara's phone lit up with Sameer's name. He was waiting for his taxi, and he seized the moment to call her. Her voice, warm and familiar, filled the air the moment she answered.

"Hey, did you miss me during your journey?" she asked, a playful innocence that made her words dance between them. He smiled softly, his thoughts drifting to the purity of her voice. The innocence in her voice is what makes her most beautiful, he mused. There was something about her—so unpretentious, so unafraid to be herself. In a world full of masks, she was a rare gem, a quiet, unassuming light.

"Baby, well, that's indeed a very difficult question," he replied, his voice laced with warmth. "Honestly, I did."

She paused, a quiet disbelief in her tone. "Seriously?"

"Yes," he said, his heart lifting with each word. "When the flight took off, I wished you were there to hold my hand. When the attendant served the meal, I wished we could share it, laugh, and talk about everything, like we always do. The journey would've felt lighter with you beside me. But as the minutes turned into hours and the world outside faded into the hum of the plane, the monotony slowly crept in, and I found myself drifting into sleep."

Her laughter, soft and carefree, floated to him through the phone, like a melody he had missed. It was contagious, and before he knew it, he was chuckling too, the sound bubbling up from deep within him. In that moment, amidst the miles that stretched between them, he felt the warmth of her presence, as if she were right there beside him, sharing in the simplicity of the moment. He paused, momentarily distracted by the honking of a taxi pulling up to the curb. Checking the number, he waved to signal the driver. Once inside, he rattled off his destination and settled back into the seat, his mind already drifting back to Kiara. Their conversation flowed effortlessly, a continuous thread of connection weaving between them, even across the distance. Amidst the chatter, one topic stood out—how they would stay in touch. He laid it out simply, his voice steady but warm. "You message me 'Hi' whenever you feel like talking, and I'll try to call you back if I'm not too caught up. If I don't call back right away, don't worry—I'm probably just busy, but I'll ring you later."

She smiled, impressed by the thoughtfulness in his words. She realized that he wasn't one of those people who spoke grandly but acted little; no, he was different. He approached everything with careful consideration, weighing the pros and cons, making logical decisions.

Surely missing the flight wasn't a logical one yet charming. It was the kind of thing that made her heart flutter—a reminder that love wasn't always about grand gestures, but about the small, sincere ones that showed someone truly cared. It was every girl's dream, after all, to be swept away by affection, to feel like the star of a fairy tale where the "prince charming" swept her off her feet and she lived "happily ever after." But real life wasn't a fairy tale, and she knew that. Still, she couldn't help but feel a twinge of magic every time they spoke. The long, bumpy ride from the airport to his home felt surprisingly smooth, like the distance between them had evaporated as they continued talking. Nearly an hour had passed, and by the time he reached his place, the time had come to say goodbye. He asked for a kiss, his voice soft yet playful. She felt a rush of warmth to her cheeks, her shyness creeping in. She kissed him through the phone and giggled at the awkwardness of it.

"Hey, did you? I didn't hear anything. I'm about to enter my home. Give me a real kiss. Make some sound, my sunshine." His teasing tone made her laugh even harder.

Her giggle turned into a burst of laughter, full of innocence and joy, as if her very spirit was caught in the moment. It was this lively cocktail of his charm and her pure heart that stirred something between them—a playful, lively energy that only grew stronger with every word. After a few shy and funny attempts from her, she finally managed to speak, still chuckling. "I really have to get back to work. You take care."

He smiled, kissing her through the phone once more, his voice soft but sincere. "Okay, baby, take care."

And with that, they hung up, both carrying a piece of the other in their hearts.

After disconnecting his call, she let out a deep breath and smiled to herself. She opened her laptop, already burdened with the heaps of work that had piled up during the day. The moment she clicked open her mailbox, a flood of new emails bombarded her inbox, pushing it to the brink of crashing. It appears everyone knew the tumultuous path she was walking and had decided to add to the mess. With a sigh, she dove into the sea of messages, sorting through them one by one. Three hours later, she finally cleared the last of the emails, the clock now showing the late evening hours. Exhausted, she leaned back in her chair, only to be jolted upright by the ringing phone. An urgent client call was waiting. The next hour slipped by in a blur of concerns and explanations as the customer, frustrated with the delivered solution, vented their displeasure. But she kept her calm, patiently addressed the issues, and diffused all his concerns. As the call ended, her mind still buzzing with the aftermath, the quality manager's voice came through with a compliment that made her heart swell.

"You are very impressive, Kiara," he said. "Nowadays, I've seen very few young people with such strong convincing power! Keep it up."

Her face lit up with satisfaction and happiness, the weight of the day momentarily forgotten. Despite the chaos and exhaustion, she had made it through, and the recognition was the perfect reward. It was moments like these that made her believe in her own strength.

As she leaned back, Manoj bought the dinner to her room.

"Ma'am, where is sir?"

"Sir. He has gone to Mumbai. He will be back in a week's time."

"Ok. How are you feeling now."

"I am good."

Manoj's smile was innocent, almost too innocent for her to fully comprehend. He had placed the tray of food on the table, his eyes meeting hers for a moment before he left the room without saying another word. She stood there for a moment, confused, yet comforted by the subtle change she had noticed in him. Once distant and somewhat aloof, Manoj had recently become more caring, more present in ways she hadn't expected. It was as though, overnight, he had transformed into someone completely different—someone she could trust, someone who genuinely cared. It was a change that felt strange yet comforting. After finishing her dinner alone in the guesthouse room, she decided to go for a walk. The night air in Chennai was warm, the kind that carried the promise of stories untold. As she wandered down the streets, she marvelled at how much this city had become a part of her. Every turn, every narrow alleyway seemed to tell her a story, but it was the newly discovered roads that fascinated her the most. They were the roads she had stumbled upon during one of her walks with Sameer—one of their lazy evening strolls that had slowly become a tradition. How strange it felt to walk them now, without him beside her. The very path seemed to hum with memories of their time together, and she couldn't help but feel a quiet ache in her chest as she retraced their steps. The breeze brushed against her skin, carrying with it the familiar scents of the city—fresh jasmine, dust from the streets, and the distant sound of honking horns. As she walked, her mind wandered, thinking back to all the decisions she had made in life, to the moments of doubt, and the moments of triumph. She had fought so hard to get here. To this place. She had faced countless obstacles, but with each one, she had learned and grown. She had achieved things she never thought possible. And yet, there was still so much more waiting for her. The future felt vast and full of promise, but it was hard to shake the feeling of loneliness that had begun to creep in. As if on cue, her phone buzzed in her pocket, snapping her from her thoughts. She fished it out quickly, seeing his name flash across the screen.

Without hesitation, she answered, her breath catching as she heard his familiar voice on the other end.

"Goodnight, baby," he said, his tone softer than usual, almost whispering through the phone. "I won't be able to talk today."

She blinked, surprised by the abruptness of the call. "Ok, take…" she began, but before she could finish, the line went dead.

For a moment, anger and frustration bubbled up within her—how could he hang up so quickly? How could he not let her say more? Yet, in the silence that followed, a wave of warmth flooded her heart. He had called. He had made the effort. In that short exchange, she felt special, wanted. It wasn't about the length of the conversation, but about the emotion behind it.

His husky voice lingered in her mind, and she imagined his rough yet endearing face, the one she had come to know so well. She imagined him standing there, his hands gently running through her hair, his lips brushing her forehead in that way only he could. The cool breeze seemed to carry his touch, and she could almost see the light in his eyes, the love and warmth that radiated from him whenever he was close. But even with these thoughts, there was a slight emptiness, an echo of something missing. She exhaled slowly, shaking off the feeling. Just a few more days, she reminded herself. Soon, they would be together again, and all would feel right in the world. With a sigh, she returned to the guesthouse. The familiar, quiet room greeted her, but her thoughts lingered on the call, on Sameer, on the strange tug in her chest. She dropped her clothes on the chair by the bed and sat down, picking up her phone to check her emails. But fatigue overtook her quickly, and before she realized it, she drifted to sleep. It was the most peaceful sleep she had in months. No restless tossing, no yearning for his presence by her side. Just deep, undisturbed rest. She awoke the next morning with a sense of calm she hadn't felt in a long time. Maybe it was the quiet of the night, or maybe, it was the realization that no matter where life took her, she was on her way to something bigger. Something even better.

The weather that morning was unusually pleasant, with a soft breeze brushing against the windows. Yet, as she made her way to the breakfast table, she found herself alone. The usual clinking of cups and chatter was absent, and there was no one to greet her with a warm "Good morning." The newspaper lay untouched on the center table in the living area, and for a moment, she considered asking someone, "Could you please lend me the newspaper?" But there was no one. No one to share this quiet, lonely moment with. She wasn't sure what she was feeling. On one hand, she felt a sharp pang of solitude. On the other hand, there was an undeniable sense of happiness bubbling inside her. She had found someone who loved her wholeheartedly, who cared for her deeply, and that should have been enough, shouldn't it? Still, there was something unsettling about the emptiness in the space around her, the silence that felt more profound than ever. She finished her breakfast quickly, clearing the table before grabbing her bag and heading out for work. The day was already shaping up to be overwhelming. The office greeted her with a mountain of tasks, each one more urgent than the last. There was no breathing space, no moment to think or even pause. With each passing hour, her schedule became tighter, more packed. Meetings after meetings, endless emails, and the relentless ticking of the clock left her feeling suffocated. She couldn't afford to stop.

She didn't have time for anything other than work. Sameer had messaged her several times throughout the day on Google Messenger, but between one meeting and another, she barely had the time to look at her phone. When she did, she often found herself responding half-heartedly, just a quick, "I'm busy, talk later" or "Sorry, can't chat right now." It felt like the week, which had started with so much promise, had slipped away into chaos. The texts, the calls, the moments they shared seemed so far away now, buried under the weight of deadlines and expectations. By late afternoon, the pressure was starting to get to her. There was a string of messages from Sameer. Her heart skipped a beat as she read through them carefully now, the words cutting through her exhaustion like a sharp knife.

"Where are you? Why aren't you responding? We shouldn't have taken our relationship to such a level when you weren't sure! I apologize if I did something wrong."

The messages hit her harder than she expected. Her stomach twisted with guilt, and suddenly, the risks of her project seemed distant and insignificant. The risks to her relationship felt far more pressing. She had to call him back—immediately. She excused herself from the meeting room, telling her colleagues it was an emergency. She stepped out into the hallway, her heart racing as she made her way to the washroom. There, closing the door, she dialled his number. When he picked up, his voice was rough, hoarse—as if he had been crying or had a cold. A mixture of both, as she would later find out. The sound of his voice, laden with emotion, made her heart ache.

"Hey, I'm really sorry that I couldn't respond," she said quickly, trying to calm him. She explained the situation—how hectic her work had been, how she barely had time for herself.

"I'm sorry," he repeated, his voice filled with frustration and hurt. "It's just… I was so worried. I didn't know where you were or what was going on."

She tried to soothe him, "If you call me after 7 p.m., I'll be in a better position to talk. I promise."

"Okay, I'll try," he said, his tone softening.

Before she could say anything else, she kissed the phone screen, her voice tender, "Now, I have to go. I'm really sure about this, about us."

He chuckled, and for a moment, everything felt right again. She smiled, feeling reassured by the familiar warmth of their connection.

As she returned to the meeting room, her colleagues gave her strange looks. They knew it wasn't an emergency, and they couldn't help but raise an eyebrow at her quick exit. She sat down, joining the conversation, and by the time the meeting wrapped up and everyone had aligned, the clock struck 7:00 p.m.

"I'm so tired," she sighed to her colleagues, rubbing her temples. Just as she said the words, her phone rang. The dismay on her face transformed into a wide grin as she picked up the call.

"Hello," she answered, her voice light.

On the other end, Sameer was in the men's changing room at his apartment complex. The sound of water splashing and people talking in the background made it clear that his wife and kids were swimming outside. He didn't want to talk in front of them, so he had retreated to a more private space.

"I was so anxious," he confessed, his voice still carrying the remnants of his earlier tension. "When you didn't reply, I wondered... I wondered if you were distancing yourself."

She felt guilty, but also strangely comforted by the fact that he cared so much. She reassured him again, explaining the chaos of her day, and after a few more moments of conversation, he seemed to calm down.

He kissed her multiple times through the phone, and she couldn't help but smile, her heart lightening. "Isn't someone in the changing room laughing at you?" she teased.

He ignored the question, his voice still soft. "Do you know how to swim?"

She paused for a moment, then answered honestly, "No, but I can learn if you agree to teach me."

"Sure, Darling. We'll see about that."

As the conversation continued, she couldn't help but feel a deep sense of contentment. Their happiness echoed in the form of laughter that filled the spaces between their words, a laughter that seemed to resonate deeply in their hearts. The conversation stretched on, as he shared little details of his day after reaching home—his wife's latest shopping spree, and his son's endless rants about new toys and school friends. It was all mundane, yet to him, these were the things that filled his life. She listened, but her mind was elsewhere. She could feel the weight of his words, but it didn't matter. She wasn't interested in the details of his family's day. The connection between them was too powerful to let such things distract her. Instead, with a quiet breath, she interrupted his rambling.

"I'm not able to sleep at night," she said softly. "I'm just thinking about us. You aren't letting me sleep. I'm eagerly waiting for you to come back and hold me."

He fell silent for a moment, understanding the subtle message she had delivered. She didn't need to hear about his wife or son; she needed him. He was an intelligent man, and he knew better than to press her further about the details of his day. He didn't feel the need to question her or defend his life, because in that moment, he understood the desire in her words. Rather than being offended or annoyed, he simply responded with a kiss—a gesture that spoke volumes, filling the space between them with affection and care. The words they exchanged seemed to bridge the distance between them, bringing them closer even though miles apart. She felt as though a once-closed part of her heart, one that had been bruised and battered, was slowly healing. Each conversation with him seemed to smooth over the cracks, replacing the old pain with something new, something bright. They had formed a bond, one that was becoming unbreakable despite the obstacles in their way. Though neither of them wanted the conversation to end, reality tugged them both back. They knew they had to say goodbye, but there was reluctance in their words. Neither wanted to hang up, but they did, reluctantly, knowing that their lives would soon have to go on.

Kiara gathered herself for the day ahead and left the office, heading toward her guest house. It wasn't far, and for once, she decided against taking the usual office cab. Instead, she walked, allowing herself the rare opportunity to enjoy some "me" time. It was a time for reflection and to relive the memories she had begun to build with him, the laughter, the sweet words, the gentle affection that now filled her heart. She missed him, no doubt. She missed the feel of his voice, the sound of his laughter. But at the same time, she found solace in their small, everyday conversations. Their connection, even though via phone and messenger, felt real. Every message, every call, brought them closer together. With each conversation, they both fell deeper in love.

It was true what they said, "Distance makes the heart grow fonder."

She had always been sceptical of such adages, dismissing them as oversimplified truths. But now, as she walked the familiar streets, those words seemed to ring louder in her mind. Perhaps it was because the distance between them had made her realize just how much he cared, how much she wanted him. Sometimes, it was as though the space between them only deepened their connection, making it feel more powerful with each passing day. Her phone beeped suddenly, pulling her out of her thoughts. She glanced at the screen, seeing a new message from him.

"I love you."

The message lingered in her mind long after she had read it. She smiled quietly, feeling a warmth spread through her chest. In that moment, all the miles between them didn't seem as important. She wasn't alone; not anymore. And no matter how far apart they were, their hearts were connected in ways that words alone could never explain. Her fingers hovered over the keypad as she prepared to reply to his message, but as her eyes scanned the screen, they stopped. Another message from him had just popped up, and the words left her feeling frustrated.

"My wife is near, so don't reply."

There was a sudden wave of confusion and unease. She stared at the screen, the weight of his words pressing down on her. Don't reply. It was as if he was asking her to suppress her feelings, to hide her thoughts. She had been so eager to tell him how much she loved him, how much she missed him, but now... Why was he telling her not to reply? Her mind began to race, the reality of their situation settling in like a stone in her stomach. Am I doing something wrong? she wondered. For long, she had convinced herself that this love, this connection, was something special. But now, standing at the edge of it all, she questioned whether she was losing herself in it. She thought about the girl she used to be—the one who, after ages of feeling detached from her emotions, had finally allowed herself to fall in love again. The one who could distinguish between the tingling feeling of love and the discomfort of uncertainty. But now, that very same love seemed to be drowning her in doubt. Is this right? The reality of falling in love with a married man began to rear its ugly head, and it was harder to ignore than before. At the beginning, when everything was new and intoxicating, she had been blinded by the depth of her feelings. She didn't think about his family, about his commitments. All that mattered to her was the connection they shared—the intimacy, the late-night talks, the stolen moments. But now, as her emotions grew stronger, she couldn't help but wonder about the consequences. What will this lead to? There was a constant tug-of-war inside her—like a battle between two forces, neither of which was willing to give in. The voice of the angel in her mind, though weak, whispered a reminder that she was committing a sin. This isn't right. He has a family. What if he leaves them for you? The thought made her stomach turn. The idea of breaking apart someone else's home, of causing pain and destruction, was unbearable. But then, there was the devil—the voice that was far more forceful, more persuasive. It sneered at her hesitation, urging her to push forward. Everything is fair in love and war. It was a mantra that seemed to echo louder the more conflicted she felt. Why should she deny herself happiness because of a set of rules she didn't believe in? If they were both happy, if they both felt alive in each other's presence, wasn't that enough?

She clutched her phone tighter, torn between the two conflicting voices. The angel and the devil fought inside her, pulling her in different directions. As she sat there, caught in the whirlwind of her thoughts, she knew she couldn't stay in this place forever. Something had to give. She could either let this love consume her and face the consequences, or she could walk away, leaving behind the one thing that had made her feel alive in ways she hadn't thought possible. But for now, she did nothing. She just stared at the screen, unsure of what her next move should be. Should she ignore the angel's whispers and listen to the devil's promises of freedom? Or should she stop everything before it went too far, too deep, and saved herself from the inevitable heartbreak?

She couldn't help but wonder if she had finally found the man of her dreams—the one who loved her the way she had always imagined. Isn't that more important? she asked herself. The complexities of life seemed to melt away in the warmth of his affection. She had been swept up by the idea of love, by the passion that connected them, but now, the shadows of doubt crept in. What was right and what was wrong? Who defines them? Wasn't love above all else? These were the questions that echoed in her mind as she stood on the precipice, torn between the love that felt so real and the knowledge of its potential consequences. The rational part of her, the voice that had once guided her through difficult decisions, now seemed to quiet in the presence of the intoxicating pull of his love.

In the quiet moments that followed, she knew one thing for sure: This battle wasn't over.

She reached the guest house, the familiar four walls that had become her temporary sanctuary. The day had been a blur, filled with emails and meetings, and the complexity of love, all weighed heavily on her. She went through the motions of her evening routine, putting on her favourite pink t-shirt and oversized off-white pyjama, the ones that always made her feel cozy and safe. She nibbled on her dinner, half-focused as she sifted through work emails. The next few days were going to be chaotic, filled with the final preparations for the project closure, and she wasn't sure how she was going to balance it all. Her workload, already immense, seemed to grow with each passing hour. But it wasn't just the pressure of work that made her anxious. It was the strange relationship she found herself in, the conflicting emotions that surged through her, making every moment feel both thrilling and terrifying. Sitting in her favourite corner of the bed, cushioned by soft pillows and with the AC blowing cool air around her, she tried to calm her racing thoughts. The exhaustion from the day, combined with the emotional turmoil, made her eyes heavy. Despite her attempts to stay awake, sleep claimed her, pulling her into its comforting embrace.

The next morning, she woke up early, just as she had every other day, completing her daily chores with mechanical precision. There was a dullness to it now—a monotony that had crept into her routine ever since he had come into her life. Without him by her side, everything felt distant, unemotional. Even the simplest tasks seemed to lose their meaning. Her heart ached in his absence. The days felt longer, colder, and more lifeless. She finished getting ready, leaving for work at approximately 7:15 a.m., the empty space beside her in the bed was a constant reminder of his absence. It was as if a part of her was missing, the part that had come alive when they were together. The joy, the laughter, the connection—it all seemed to dissipate when he wasn't around. The love she felt for Sameer was undeniable, but the weight of the consequences and the doubts in her mind were beginning to take their toll. How could she balance her feelings with her responsibilities? How could she stay true to herself when everything around her seemed so chaotic? She didn't have the answers yet. All she knew was that the journey ahead would be filled with difficult decisions, moments of joy, and the heartache of finding her way through it all. For now, all she could do was take it one step at a time, hoping that, eventually, the pieces of her life would fall into place.

The early morning hours at the office had always been Kiara's preferred time to work. The office was quieter, with fewer people, offering a peaceful escape from the usual buzz of chatter and interruptions. There was something comforting about the stillness—no coffee corner conversations, no distractions, just the sound of her fingers tapping away at the keyboard as she focused on the task at hand. She needed this time to prepare for the upcoming Go-live. The project was nearing its final stages, and every minute felt critical. Her mind, however, wasn't solely occupied with work. Between planning for the Go-live and managing her relationship with Sameer, there was a constant mental juggling act. Long-distance relationships, she had learned, required an enormous amount of patience, planning, and space—so much space, in fact, that it often felt like a series of careful calculations. When was the best time to call? When could they talk without either of them feeling neglected or overwhelmed? It was a delicate balance, one that sometimes felt almost as demanding as her day-to-day work life. Initially, the Go-live had been scheduled for the weekend, but in a sudden turn of events, it was moved up to Thursday night. The entire project team was informed that, if everything went according to plan, they could all fly home on Saturday evening. The news brought a sense of relief to the team, with everyone now working at double speed to meet the new deadline. For Kiara, the early success of the project meant more than just relief—it meant the end of the long, intense stretch of work. But there was also a tinge of sadness that lingered. She had been looking forward to seeing Sameer after a week of waiting, but now, with the Go-live moved earlier, the chances of meeting him were nil. He was supposed to arrive on Monday morning, but with her flight now moved to Saturday evening, the only way they could meet was if either he arrived earlier or if something went wrong with the Go-live, delaying the project. Neither option seemed likely, and the thought of not seeing him made her feel a knot of longing deep in her chest.

She wanted to tell him about the sudden change of plans—wanted to reach out and make sure he understood why she wouldn't be able to meet him—but the "no communication" rule that he had set up when he was at home kept her from doing so. The very same rule that had kept her from sharing her day-to-day thoughts and frustrations with him when he was with his family. It was a policy she understood, but it was also a policy that sometimes felt like a prison for her heart. She hesitated. There was nothing she could do to change the situation, no way to alter the course of events. So, she decided to wait for his call. And then, just as the evening began to settle in, the familiar ping of a message broke the silence of her thoughts. As she saw the notification pop up on her laptop screen, she thought, "I hope it's from Sameer," with a small smile tugging at her lips.

Her prayers, it seemed, had been answered. It was him. As always, his message was simple, but filled with affection:

"How is my baby doing?"

Her heart warmed at the words, the familiar tone of his voice coming through even in text. For a moment, all the chaos of the day—the looming pressure of the Go-live, the distance between them, the uncertainty of when they would see each other again—melted away. All that mattered was that he was thinking of her. The words she had been dying to say rushed to her mind, but she took a deep breath before responding.

She typed back, smiling to herself as she did. She stared at the screen, her fingers hovering over the keyboard as she tried to find the right words. The change of plans had thrown her into disarray, and she needed to tell him, needed to share this moment of uncertainty with the one person who always seemed to have the right words to make things feel better. She typed out her message slowly, letting the words sink in as they appeared on the screen.

"I am fine but there is an issue here. There is a change of plans now. If the Go-live is successful today, then I've to travel back on Saturday."

The seconds that followed felt endless. She could almost feel the weight of the silence between them, as if every word she had sent out was hanging in the air, unanswered. She waited. Her eyes fixed on the blinking cursor, waiting for his reply to come through.

Finally, after what felt like an eternity, his message appeared. But it wasn't what she had expected.

"I don't know what to say but somehow, when I was leaving, I had the feeling that we'll not be able to meet again, at least in Chennai."

"It was my sixth sense that gave me an inkling of the impending disaster. It was again one of the reasons that I missed my flight and returned to you to express my love. Even when I left for Mumbai, I felt as if I'm leaving someone behind forever."

The words hit her like a tidal wave, crashing against her resolve.

Tears sprang to her eyes as she read his message, and she quickly wiped them away, trying to keep her composure. She was in the office, surrounded by colleagues, and the last thing she wanted was to break down in front of them. But despite her best efforts, the emotion welled up inside her. The office, the people, the busy hum of activity—all of it seemed to fade away. All that remained was the cold weight of his words. He had sensed the impending separation, the distance between them, and it had hurt him just as much as it hurt her. The realization that they both felt the same way, even without saying the words aloud, struck her deeply. Yet, despite the shared pain, there was still the undeniable truth: she had to go back. She had no control over the situation. The Go-live had to be completed, and she need to leave post that. She had to fight the sinking feeling in her chest and keep going.

To try and comfort him, she sent a message, "You know I have lost every inch of fat from my body. My body is demanding a wholesome North Indian meal!"

His response was quick, laced with the familiar tone of concern: "Don't try to be funny."

A small smile tugged at Kiara's lips as she read his words. Despite the heaviness in her heart, the familiar banter between them was a reminder that, even in the midst of everything, they still had each other's support.

"Listen," he typed back, "I don't know when, but we will meet soon. Just not in Chennai."

And with that, a small sense of peace settled over her, knowing that despite the uncertainty, they would find their way to each other. It might not be now, it might not be soon, but it would happen. Both allowed themselves to hold on to that hope. As the office around her buzzed with activity, she sat back in her chair, breathing in deeply. The journey ahead was uncertain, but one thing was clear: no matter the distance, no matter the obstacles, she would find her way back to him. And when that day came, it would be everything. The conversation between them despite the uncertainty and underlying tension, had ended in a strange, unspoken reassurance. They both weren't happy with where things were heading, but they had tried, in their own way, to console and comfort each other. This was love, she thought—offering support and reassurance when neither of them knew what the future held.

A distant memory surfaced in her mind—Jack and Rose from Titanic, desperately holding on to each other after the ship had sunk. She smiled wistfully. That's how love works, she mused, even when you aren't sure about anything else. If you don't stand by each other, through the good and bad, then is it truly love? With a small chuckle, she added in her head, if they could express their love in a sinking ship, in a freezing ocean, surely, we can also figure this out.

For now, though, the only way to express any semblance of affection was through emoticons. It might sound silly, and yet, in this age of digital relationships, it was the best they could do. She kissed him virtually, the little digital heart symbol lighting up on the screen, before she sent it off. That's how long-distance relationships work in the digital age, she thought to herself, and sighed. She had never really been in a "relationship" before meeting him, so she could only guess at what it truly meant to navigate the complexities of love from miles away. With the unwanted goodbye, she returned to her work, though a part of her was still lingering in the emotional fog they'd both created. The next few hours were a blur of tasks and systems. She poured her energy into the final checks, making sure everything was working smoothly, that the upgraded systems were behaving as expected, and that everything was in place for the project success. As the servers finally went online, and users began testing the new configurations, the feedback was overwhelmingly positive. To her surprise, only a couple of minor issues were reported - issues that she could easily address. It was a success, and she felt a rush of pride wash over her.

But as the congratulatory emails flooded in, from her peers, managers, and stakeholders, she found herself feeling hollow. She had pulled off a significant achievement, but her heart wasn't in it. Sure, the accolades were deserved, but they felt empty. The feeling of accomplishment was overshadowed by the gnawing emptiness that came from knowing she wouldn't see him any time soon. She had always believed that success would be enough, that achieving her career goals would bring her fulfilment. But today, she realized that even professional triumphs couldn't fill the space that was left when love was missing. Such is the paradox of life, she thought bitterly. The same girl who had once dreamed of a spotless career, who had worked tirelessly for this very success, was now unable to fully enjoy it. Her project had been flawless, and her reputation had been solidified with the project success. Yet she felt empty. The clock kept ticking, indifferent to her internal turmoil. It was quarter to four in the morning—late, even for her. She stared at the screen, watching the cursor blink back at her. Time didn't care about love or heartbreak, success or failure. It moved forward relentlessly, leaving her little space to breathe. As the hours passed, her colleagues, who had been involved in the project, congratulated each other before packing their bags and heading home for the night. The office was beginning to empty out, and she found herself sitting alone at her desk. The quiet of the office, with everyone else gone, made her feel even more alone. She packed her things and left the office, stepping into the stillness of the night. The walk to her guest house was quiet, the streets deserted, and she couldn't help but think that, despite everything, nothing felt complete without him beside her. When she reached her temporary home, she was exhausted. She'd spent hours working through the final checks, barely giving herself a break. But now, with the end of the project behind her and no immediate work left, she had time to think.

As she entered her room, the weight of everything seemed to hit her all at once. The bright, successful career that she had built, the distant love she was nurturing, and the emptiness that filled the space in between—it all felt like too much, yet somehow, not enough. She dropped her things on the bed and looked out the window at the quiet streets. She longed for the simplicity of the past few weeks—when work was challenging but manageable, and when Sameer's calls were her only distraction. Now, she had everything she'd wanted professionally, and yet, it wasn't enough. Perhaps that was the cruellest part of life—the realization that no matter how much you achieve, there are parts of your soul that remain unfulfilled.

It was the final day in Chennai, and she couldn't shake the strange feeling that had settled over her. Was she happy? Was she sad? She had so many plans, so many expectations, but destiny had led her in a direction she hadn't anticipated. "My life has turned topsy-turvy," she thought as she made her way to the office, the familiar streets of Chennai slipping by in a blur. She arrived earlier than usual, a sense of urgency pulling her forward. Her tickets were booked for 8:00 a.m. the next day. Her colleagues back in Gurgaon were excited to have her return. After finishing her tasks, she left the office and returned to the guest house. The end of this chapter of her life felt hollow. She packed her bags, cleared her bills for food and laundry, and went for a walk around the same streets she had discovered with Sameer. They had shared so many memories here—long walks, deep conversations, and fleeting moments of happiness. Even though he wasn't physically present, walking those streets made her feel as though he was with her. He was always with her, deep inside her heart. She went to the same ice cream place they had visited together and ordered his favourite flavour. The little indulgence was a small tribute to their love. Love makes you do things you don't particularly enjoy, but you still do it just to feel closer to the person you love, she thought as she savoured the creamy sweetness. The evening that followed was quiet and introspective. Alone in her room, she sifted through memories, replaying the moments of joy and laughter they had shared, feeling both grateful and heartbroken. She lay down, feeling a weight in her chest, her thoughts racing, but eventually, sleep claimed her. The next morning came too soon. It was uneventful—no grand farewell, no last-minute miracle. Sameer hadn't shown up. He had never promised to, but there was a part of her that had still hoped for a miracle. With a heavy heart, she made her way to the airport.

As she stepped out of the guest house, she felt an unfamiliar pang of loss. It wasn't him she was leaving behind this time. No, this time, it was Manoj, the housekeeping staff. He had witnessed her journey in Chennai, the blossoming of a love that had changed her in ways she hadn't expected. They had shared small conversations, smiles, and quiet moments. Now, it was time to say goodbye. She knocked on the kitchen door, and Manoj opened it, his eyes unexpectedly moist.

She pulled him into a tight hug, a simple gesture that spoke volumes of their shared experience. "Bhaiya, we will meet soon," she said softly, her voice thick with emotion. They exchanged numbers, a small promise that they weren't strangers anymore. With a final, lingering hug, she bid him farewell. The airport loomed ahead, but her heart felt fuller than before. She wasn't entirely alone in this world; there were people, even in the most unexpected places, who had shared a piece of her life. Once she reached the airport, she called Rehan. The excitement in his voice was palpable. "Hey, I'm at the airport, and I'm finally coming back. Can you believe it?" She said, trying to match his upbeat energy. Rehan teased her as he always did.

"I don't trust you, superwoman! Till the flight takes off, lands in Gurgaon, and I see you at the office, I'm not going to believe it." His voice was playful, but Kiara could hear the excitement bubbling underneath.

Laughing, she mimicked his voice in a funny way, and they both erupted in laughter. It felt so good to laugh again, to feel that lightness, even if just for a moment. The sounds of their laughter echoed through the airport, and she didn't even care that people were staring. The noise, the attention, none of it mattered. This was her moment, a small break from the weight of the world on her shoulders.

"Bye, see you soon, Rehan," she said, feeling lighter now, even as the reality of leaving Chennai sank in.

The flight home was just the beginning of another chapter. But for now, she smiled, knowing that even though her journey in Chennai had ended, it had shaped her in ways she couldn't yet fully comprehend.

> "*As my heart stretched across the miles, so did my confidence, both in love and in work. Each success, whether near or far, became a step towards something greater.*"
>
> – *Unknown*

Gurgaon, 2011

In the Space between us

The flight from Chennai to Delhi had been uneventful, a quiet and monotonous experience. There were no delays, no turbulence, and certainly no distractions. As the plane touched down at Indira Gandhi International Airport, Kiara felt a strange sense of relief. She was closer to home now, closer to the familiar chaos of her daily life. Waiting for her luggage at the baggage claim, her mind wandered back to Chennai. The city, the memories, and the feeling of love she had left behind there were still fresh in her mind. She smiled to herself, thinking, Naive! How quickly she had fallen into the whirlpool of emotions, without really knowing what she was diving into. It had been an adventure; one she wouldn't never forget. Exiting the airport, the dry, hot air hit her face with an almost aggressive force. The winds ruffled her well-kept hair, and the sun's harsh rays seemed to penetrate her sunglasses. She squinted for a moment but didn't care. The pollution, the hustle of the city, the noisy streets—everything was so different from the calm of Chennai, yet somehow it felt oddly comforting. It was like returning to a version of herself she had abandoned for a while. She made her way to the pre-paid taxi counter, a slight grin playing on her lips as she thought, Now I'll be able to gorge on Sev puri and chaat. Her cravings for home were intense, and the thought of indulging in the familiar street food brought her some comfort. Soon, the cab arrived. She loaded her luggage into the boot, her mind still mulling over the past few weeks. Without Sameer beside her, without anyone to talk to, to share her thoughts, she felt oddly isolated. The hum of the engine and the Bollywood numbers playing on the radio didn't hold her attention. The passing houses, the crowded streets, and the scenery were just a blur outside her window. Back to the grind, she sighed to herself, rolling her eyes as the cab weaved through traffic. It was strange to think that just days ago, she had been caught up in the excitement and chaos of the work, the last-minute changes, the never-ending work, and of course, the love that had bloomed in unexpected places. Now, she was heading back to the routine she had known before—just another day in the life.

Her phone buzzed in her pocket, interrupting her thoughts. She glanced at the screen to see if it's a message from Sameer. But it wasn't. She quickly pushed aside the faint hope that fluttered in her chest. They had shared so much, yet now they were miles apart, separated by the reality of their respective lives. She quickly shoved the phone back into her bag, unsure if she was ready to face the emotional turbulence that awaited her when they spoke again. As the cab sped towards Gurgaon, the cityscape shifting outside, she couldn't shake the feeling of displacement. But for now, as she approached the familiar streets of Gurgaon, Kiara decided to push those thoughts aside. She had survived the whirlwind of the past few months, and now it was time to focus on what was in front of her. One step at a time, she thought, rolling the window down to let the cool evening breeze rush in. By the time she reached her PG, it was already afternoon.

She let out a quiet sigh, disappointment settling in her chest as she stared at the empty screen of her phone. She had hoped for a message from him, something to bridge the gap between their worlds, but the silence only made her feel more isolated. The distance, though just a few hundred kilometres, seemed endless in moments like this. She lay back down, her phone still resting in her hand, staring at the ceiling as her mind drifted. The lack of his familiar messages or calls left a hole in her that no amount of work or distractions could fill. After a moment, she set the phone down beside her and decided to give herself a break from thinking about it. Closing her eyes, she let the exhaustion take over again, but this time, the sleep was interrupted by the familiar sound of a vibration. Her eyes snapped open, and she quickly reached for the phone, hoping this time it was him.

The screen lit up with a message, and her heart welled with happiness when she saw his name.

"Hey bunny! How was the flight?"

A smile quickly formed on her lips, and warmth spread throughout her body. She quickly typed back, her fingers moving faster than usual.

"It was fine. Just glad to be back but missing you. A lot."

"I miss you too, more than you know."

Her chest tightened with the sweet sincerity in his words. Despite the distance, the lack of physical presence, it was moments like this that reminded her how real and deep their connection was. She took a deep breath, her heart swelling with the familiar mix of joy and sadness. The uncertainty of their future, the waiting, and the longing were all worth it because in these small moments, they had something special—something real.

"I wish you were here," she replied, her fingers lingering over the keys as she hesitated for a moment. She knew he couldn't be, but she needed him to know how much she wished it.

A few seconds passed before his message appeared on the screen.

"I know. But we will be together soon. Promise."

Her smile widened; the weight of her loneliness momentarily lifted. For now, his words were enough to soothe the ache in her heart. She settled back into her bed, holding the phone close to her chest as she let herself drift back to sleep. Though the distance remained, there was a comfort in knowing that he was just a message away, and that made all the difference in the world. Immediately, her phone started ringing. She glanced at the screen, her breath catching as she saw his name light up. "Hey, my sunshine," he said, his voice felt like a melody she had come to cherish. She smiled softly, her heart skipping a beat.

"I came down to talk to you; am sitting in the car," he continued. She smiled, though there was a hint of something more in her chest—a pang of guilt, of longing, and a strange sadness. What Sameer said seemed innocent, but in reality, they were both deceiving each other. Not just the world, but themselves. They were playing a game that neither of them could truly win. She shifted the conversation, asking about his tennis match. "I won," he said with a note of pride, but his voice softened almost immediately, as if something else mattered more. "I'm really happy—not because I won, but because my son was there watching me. I'm trying to develop his interest in tennis too."

She felt the familiar ache in her chest. She didn't want to hear about his son, didn't want to think about the family he had that she could never be a part of. She didn't express her discomfort, but her mind quickly changed the subject, veering to the plans for the evening. It was easier that way—ignoring the ache, pretending that their love could exist without complications. Sometimes, it was better to stay silent. You never knew how the other person would react to your true feelings. And as far as she knew, he loved his son more than anything. How could she challenge that? How could she even dare to ask for more? He asked her what she had planned for the night, and she teased, "Are you kidding? Have you forgotten what day it is?"

His laugh was instant, light, and full of affection. "Oh, yes, I remember now! We are going to watch the World Cup finals together, but from different locations."

"Yeah," she answered, a mischievous sparkle in her eyes. "You've grown old, you know."

He laughed again; his voice filled with warmth. "Come on, baby! I'm not that old for you."

Her lips curled into a teasing smile. "I don't know," she said with an evil laugh, the playfulness covering the ache beneath her words.

"Don't worry," he assured her, his tone softening. "I won't leave you alone. I'll call you during the match." Then, with a sigh, he added, "It's already been ten minutes. I need to rush home. I'm running late. Can I call you later?"

She made a face, but inside, she understood. He had to go. She had no other choice but to agree, though the emptiness that filled her once the call ended was undeniable. After disconnecting, she walked to the kitchen and began preparing hot chocolate. The ritual comforted her, reminding her of the time he had made it for her—a small, intimate moment that felt like a lifetime ago. A smile briefly touched her lips, but it quickly faded. With the mug in hand, she moved to the balcony, humming "Ek Sanam Chahiye Aashiqui Ke Liye" under her breath. The cool evening breeze kissed her face, and her long silken hair flowed behind her like a dark river. It was a peaceful moment, yet her heart felt heavy. He'll never leave them for me. And even if he did, it wouldn't be right. Why can't we just have happiness in our lives? The thoughts swirled in her mind, pulling at her heart. He calls me his sunshine, but I'll never be his. Not when he belongs to someone else.

Her thoughts twisted and turned like a storm inside her. Deep down, she knew they were living a lie. The love they shared was doomed from the start, but neither of them knew how to let go. It was wrong. She knew it couldn't last. But the pull of her feelings, the need to hold on just a little longer, kept her in this twisted dance.

Why keep going? Why not just stop? she asked herself, but the answers eluded her.

A soft rain began to fall, the gentle tapping on the balcony floor mingling with the quiet sobs that escaped her. The heavens, it seemed, were crying with her. She sank into a bamboo chair, the tears blending with the rain. Her heart felt heavy, burdened with the truth that they were never meant to be.

"You must ask yourself how you want to live your life." The Dalai Lama's words resonated in her mind, but she had no response—only the profound, aching silence of a love that would never be enough.

Gurgaon, 2011

Truths We Didn't Want to Hear

Kiara was completely encapsulated in her thoughts. The soft melody of "Aahatein ho rahi hai teri" echoed faintly in the background, like a distant whisper of memories she couldn't escape. For a moment, it felt as though the world around her had faded, leaving only the music and her swirling thoughts. But soon, she realized the sound wasn't just a song—it was her phone ringing. Her heart skipped a beat, as it always did when she heard the familiar ring. There was always a certain twinkle in her eyes when her phone rang, the obvious reason being Sameer. But this time, as she glanced at the screen, it wasn't his name lighting up. It was Aniket's, her childhood friend. She felt a twinge of disappointment but quickly masked it as she answered the call.

"Hello?"

"It's been so long since we've met or even spoken," Aniket's voice came through, warm and casual, as if they had never lost touch.

"Yeah," Kiara responded, her voice lacking the enthusiasm it should have carried. The words slipped out flat, and she couldn't hide the disinterest that tinged them.

Aniket noticed. "I thought you'd be missing me, but it seems like you aren't happy to hear my voice," he teased, sensing the distance in her tone.

She quickly tried to recover. "Yaar! I'm glad you called. Yes, it's been really long! What's up?" she said, forcing a note of excitement into her voice. But the truth was far from it. She wasn't thinking about her childhood friend; her mind was elsewhere.

"Shall we meet?" Aniket's voice was full of eagerness, and it pulled her back into the present.

"I was about to say the same. Yes, we can definitely catch up at our favourite place tomorrow evening at 6:00 p.m. Right now, I'm a little caught up with a presentation, so can't talk much."

Aniket's excitement faltered, and she heard the annoyance in his tone. "Ok, fine! Let's meet tomorrow," he said curtly before disconnecting the call.

She stood there for a moment, staring at her phone, her mind still lost in the world she'd been retreating to. She hadn't even noticed the sharpness in Aniket's voice, nor how quickly he had ended the call. It didn't matter. The rain outside had resumed, and with it, the sense of melancholy that had been clinging onto her. The rain continued the next day, though not as heavily. Still, it carried the same gloominess, a constant reminder of her conflicted emotions. "You really cannot trust the weather forecast in India," she muttered to herself, her eyes drifting to the window as she watched the raindrops slide down the glass. After a slow, lazy morning, and an afternoon spent doing practically nothing, she had hoped that the rain would let up by the evening. But as the hours passed, the rain only intensified. A sigh escaped her lips. She had been looking forward to meeting Aniket, but the weather seemed determined to ruin her plans. Despite the gloomy weather, she made up her mind. She would go, rain or shine. By the time she finished getting dressed, the rain had slowed, though it wasn't entirely gone. It was just a light drizzle now, but still enough to keep the world wrapped in a blanket of Gray. She stepped outside and made her way to the nearest metro station, HUDA CITY CENTRE. She boarded the train, finding a small space in the ladies' compartment. The rhythmic clatter of the train tracks soothed her, and she plugged in her earphones, pressing play on a playlist of romantic songs. She texted Aniket to let him know she was on her way and would arrive in an hour. With the music in her ears, she sank back into her thoughts, drifting once again into her never-ending wonderland of love. Her mind wandered back to Sameer and the warmth of their shared moments, the places they had visited, the things they had talked about. She smiled softly, lost in the sweet ache of it all. The world outside the train window blurred as she retreated further into her own heart, a place where only Sameer's name echoed, a place where reality had no place.

She couldn't help but smile as she imagined Sameer and herself, moving effortlessly together in the romantic songs she played on her phone. The melodies seemed to weave around her, their lyrics painting a vivid picture of the two of them dancing, lost in the music and each other's presence. Her heart fluttered with the fantasy, and for a few moments, she was transported to a world where everything was perfect, where Sameer was hers and she was his. The thought of it was so real, so tangible, that she could almost feel the warmth of his hand on her waist and the rhythm of their steps in perfect sync. The train pulled into her destination, and she reluctantly pulled herself back to the present. She shook off the lingering daydreams, realizing it was time to face the real world again. As she deboarded the metro, she dialled Aniket's number with a sense of urgency, her thoughts still drifting between reality and fantasy.

"Thank God the rain has stopped," she thought with a small sigh of relief. The sky had cleared, and although the roads were still wet, there was a certain freshness in the air.

"Hey, late-latif! I've reached! Where are you? Still didn't leave home, I guess?" she teased, her voice light and playful, though her mind was still partly caught up in the haze of her earlier thoughts.

"I'm waiting for you at the exit gate 7 of Rajiv Chowk metro station, silly!" Aniket's voice came through, excited and eager. "This time, I'm early! Ha ha! I'm so excited that we're meeting after so long, I reached here 30 minutes ago."

Kiara chuckled, shaking her head as she walked. "OMG! Wait there, I'm walking towards you. Ahh... I think I can see you. You're wearing a green t-shirt, right?"

"Yup! But I can't see you, shorty!" Aniket replied, a grin in his voice. "Oh, wait, I spotted you!"

Kiara unplugged her earphones, her heart picking up speed. She quickened her pace, scanning the crowd, and then, in an instant, she found him. Without thinking, she jumped into his arms, hugging him tightly.

"It's so good to see you," she said, her voice muffled by his shoulder as she squeezed him tighter.

They exchanged their usual casual banter, the easy familiarity of their friendship filling the air. After a few more laughs and playful jabs, they made their way out of the station, heading straight for their favourite spot—India Gate. It had been a while since they'd come here, and Kiara was looking forward to the familiar sights and sounds that always made the place feel like home. India Gate, as always, was alive with energy. The large monument stood proudly in the distance, its stone surface glowing warmly under the fading light of the day. The surrounding area was a vibrant mix of life—shutterbugs snapping photos, families enjoying picnics, and children running around, their laughter echoing in the air. The colourful clothes of the kids created a picturesque contrast against the deep greens of the grass and the grey stone of the monument. She breathed in the air, her eyes scanning the scene around her. She loved this place, the way it was always filled with life. It was never quiet, never still. There were stalls selling ice-creams, corn, and puffed rice, the vendors calling out to the crowds with their usual enthusiasm. The buzz of activity was both comforting and exciting, as though the entire city had gathered here for a moment of joy and celebration. As she stood there, looking around at the people and the monument, she felt a sense of peace settle over her. Despite everything that had been swirling in her mind lately, India Gate always had a way of grounding her. Here, amidst the chaos, there was a quiet calm, and for a moment, she allowed herself to simply be present.

"Remember when we used to come here and sit for hours, talking about everything and nothing?" Aniket's voice interrupted her thoughts.

Kiara smiled softly, her heart lightening at the memory. "Yeah, those were the days. Seems like a lifetime ago."

But even as they reminisced, her mind couldn't help but wander back to Sameer and the dreamlike moments they had shared in Chennai. Yet, for now, India Gate had a way of keeping her rooted, offering a momentary escape from her tangled emotions. Aniket's voice buzzed on as he rambled about one thing after another—his office's latest developments, his parents' attempts to find a match for him, the disastrous habits of his new flatmate, and of course, his usual rants about politics. She nodded, half-listening, her attention drifting far from his words. Her eyes were fixed on the endless flow of people around them, the laughter of children, the chatter of families, and the distant silhouette of the India Gate. She smiled absently as Aniket continued his monologue, but inside, her mind was elsewhere. Her responses were mechanical, a simple nod here, a murmur there, enough to let him think she was engaged. But it was clear to him she wasn't. And yet, neither of them said anything. Shamelessness was the unspoken rule of their friendship. They had always shared everything with each other, good, bad, or ugly. There were no pretences. No filters. Whether or not the other person was interested didn't matter. Aniket kept talking, and she kept listening in silence. She didn't even realize that he was staring at her with an intensity she couldn't quite place.

"What?" she finally asked, her voice tinged with irritation she hadn't realized was there.

"Why are you looking at me like this?"

Aniket paused, his mouth opening and closing as if trying to find the right words.

"We share almost everything, Kiara," he began, his tone serious, "but why didn't you call me when you were in Chennai, especially during the last 2-3 weeks? Why didn't you talk about anyone you met there? You only mentioned the guesthouse and food, but nothing else."

Kiara froze. The question hung in the air, heavy and piercing. She had been expecting this, yet the words still hit her like a punch to the gut. Aniket had always been the one person who knew her well enough to see through her walls. And there was no way she could lie to him, not with the "No Lie" rule that had always governed their friendship. Tears welled up in her eyes, unbidden, as she struggled to find a response. She couldn't explain.

How could she? How could she tell him the truth without unravelling the very core of everything she had been hiding from him—and from herself? The carefree chatter that had surrounded them just moments ago felt like a distant memory. The light-heartedness of their time together was suddenly replaced with a suffocating silence. The world around them seemed to blur, as though the very ambiance of India Gate had shifted in tune with the heaviness in Kiara's chest. Aniket stared at her, clearly startled by the sudden change in atmosphere. He didn't understand what was going on. His eyes softened with confusion, but he didn't push her to speak. They both knew this wasn't a moment to be forced. She wiped her eyes hastily, trying to compose herself, but the tears kept coming. It wasn't just about the lie she was keeping from Aniket. It was everything—the tangled web of emotions she had been weaving for months. The guilt, the longing, the ache of wanting something she could never have, and the fear of admitting it to anyone, even herself. The silence stretched between them, thick and uncomfortable, until finally, Aniket broke it.

"Kiara, what's going on? What's really happening?"

She didn't answer immediately. Instead, she looked at him, her gaze clouded with unshed tears. She couldn't bear to explain, not yet. Not when it was so messy, so impossible. The truth would hurt too much—both for him and for her.

But he was patient, as he always had been with her. He waited, his eyes filled with concern, yet knowing better than to push her further. She didn't know how long they sat there, in that suspended moment between truth and silence. The world around them seemed to continue, as though unaware of the emotional storm brewing in that small corner of India Gate. It wasn't just a moment of sadness. It was a breaking point—an unravelling of something she had been holding onto for far too long. And, for the first time in what felt like forever, she allowed herself to feel it fully. The weight of the unspoken words, the guilt, the secret love that had been eating away at her inside. Her heart ached as she looked at Aniket, her emotions overflowing.

"Sorry; sorry for not understanding you," she whispered, her voice breaking.

The words felt inadequate, but it was all she could manage before she dissolved into tears. She had always been so focused on her career, so absorbed in the pursuit of academic excellence, that she never truly grasped the tender emotions that Aniket had so silently offered her over the years. Raised by her aunt, who had tormented her with cruel taunts and ridicule, Kiara had never known the warmth of a loving home. For her, returning home each day was a nightmare, a place where she felt unloved and unwanted. She buried herself in her studies, extra classes, and sports, seeking refuge in anything that kept her away from the harsh realities of her home life. Aniket, on the other hand, had entered her life in the third grade, a constant, unwavering presence. He was the charming and cute guy that every girl in school seemed to adore, and yet, he was always drawn to her. She never understood why. To her, love was a distant concept, one she had never taken seriously, not when there was so much more to worry about. Aniket, too shy to confess his feelings, chose to stay close to her as a friend, helping her with her studies and spending hours after school playing badminton or practicing for cultural events—activities he had no interest in, but endured with a quiet smile because they brought him closer to her.

Their friendship deepened over the years, and eventually, she found herself confiding in him, sharing the painful truth about her home life. Aniket listened with a kind heart, his love for her growing with every word she spoke. Raised in a stable, loving family, he couldn't fathom the cruelty she had faced, but her strength and vulnerability stirred something deep within him. He felt an overwhelming need to protect her, to shield her from all the pain she had endured. Despite the mocking whispers of their classmates, who couldn't understand their bond, Aniket and Kiara became inseparable, each other's refuge in a world that didn't quite understand them. Their relationship, though innocent and full of warmth, had no labels—no handholding, no dates, no kisses. But there was an undeniable closeness, a connection that went beyond words. Even when their paths diverged after high school, they continued to share moments, co-studying and offering support to one another. Despite their different worlds, their bond remained unbroken, a silent promise between them that no matter where life took them, they would always find their way back to each other. It wasn't that Kiara never understood his love for her; she had, many times over the years. But her ambitions, her drive to succeed, had always overshadowed those tender emotions, keeping them tucked away in the recesses of her mind. Kiara had made it to a prestigious Government Engineering college, a dream she had worked tirelessly to achieve, while Aniket continued his pursuit of becoming an Architect. Though miles apart, they stayed in touch, their bond unbroken by distance. Every day, whether through calls or messages, they continued to share their lives with each other, their conversations a steady thread that wove their worlds together. But as time passed, the delicate bud of love that had once bloomed between them never quite turned into the flower of a relationship. As the years went by, Aniket began to wonder if he could keep up his one-sided love for much longer. His heart ached, not out of anger, but out of sadness. His optimism had never paid off the way he had hoped. By the final year of college, his feelings were clear to him, but the courage to confront Kiara with them was something he had yet to summon. He dropped hints through their messages, trying to gauge her feelings, but each time, she skilfully changed the subject, never allowing the conversation to go where he so desperately wanted it to.

They say, "time heals," but Aniket knew "Time doesn't heal, it teaches you to accept and move on. Time soothes an aching heart, but never heals a broken one!"

Still, he couldn't help but joke with her. "You're in such a good college; soon you'll land a high-paying job. You'll need me, an architect, to build your mansion." They would laugh together, teasing each other about the futures they were chasing. Kiara, ever so uncomplicated in her approach to life, understood what Aniket was trying to say. She cared for him deeply, but the fears of a relationship—of losing herself in someone else's dreams—kept her from taking the leap into something more. Their bond was strong, but it was always tempered with the unspoken understanding that they could never cross the line into something deeper, no matter how much they might have wanted to. Sitting near the majestic India Gate, she couldn't hold back the flood of memories that rushed back to her. The cool evening breeze did little to soothe the heaviness in her chest. She felt a wave of guilt wash over her—guilt for the choices she had made, for the paths she had walked, and for the pain she had caused. Her mind replayed the chapters of her life that she had tried to bury, but now, they came surging back with a force she couldn't control. With a deep sigh, Kiara turned to Aniket, her eyes brimming with unshed tears.

"I need to tell you everything," she said quietly.

Her voice trembled as she began to recount what had happened during her time in Chennai. She spoke of Sameer—of their encounters, their bond, and the way he had swept her off her feet. She spared no details, even those that pained her, those that made her feel weak and foolish. He listened in silence, his heart sinking with each word she spoke.

"Sameer is married," Kiara continued, her voice barely a whisper. "He has two kids. And I don't know why… but I can't let go of him. I don't care about my future anymore, but I worry about his. I can't help how I feel. I'm so deeply and madly in love with him that I'm willing to disregard everything I've ever stood for—my own principles, my ethics… everything." Her words trailed off as tears spilled down her face, choking her voice. She wiped them away hastily, but they kept coming, uncontrollable, a torrent of regret and confusion.

He sat frozen, his gaze fixed on her, his expression unreadable, blank, and emotionless. He had never imagined that this meeting—this long-awaited moment where they would finally confront the distance that had grown between them—would turn into such a nightmarish revelation. For years, Aniket had silently loved Kiara. From the first time they met in school, his feelings for her had blossomed quietly, growing deeper with every passing day. He had always been there for her, supporting her through her struggles, even when she had turned down his indirect proposals and ridiculed the very notion of them being anything more than friends. He had swallowed his heartache, willing to remain her friend, always in the background, a constant source of support. But hearing her speak of Sameer, hearing her confess her unwavering love for someone else—someone who was already taken, who would never be hers—it shattered him in a way words couldn't describe. The silence between them stretched for what felt like an eternity. Kiara's confession hung in the air, heavy and suffocating, and Aniket was left grappling with the emotions that threatened to engulf him. His love for her had never wavered, even in the face of her obliviousness. Yet now, in the wake of her admission, he was confronted with the painful truth: she had never seen him the way he had always seen her. He was just the friend—her constant, but never the one she would choose. The thought of her loving someone else, someone who didn't even value her the way she deserved, cut him to the core. But there was nothing he could say, nothing that would change the reality of her feelings. It was a nightmare in the truest sense—a nightmare of unrequited love, of waiting patiently for a chance that would never come, and of watching someone you loved with all your heart slip further and further away. Aniket wanted to reach out to her, to comfort her, to tell her that everything would be okay—but how could he, when he was drowning in his own heartbreak? The lively scene at India Gate—the laughter of couples, the playful shouts of children, the vibrant colours of street vendors, and the cool breeze that seemed to whisper romance into the air—felt like a distant, irrelevant world to both. It was as if they were in their own bubble, one that held only pain and confusion, a stark contrast to the world around them.

She brushed away her tears, but the weight of her emotions lingered. Aniket, who had been quietly absorbing everything, slowly spoke, his voice thick with restraint. "Don't cry, Kiara," he said softly at first, but soon his words began to rise in volume, fuelled by years of suppressed emotions and frustration. Kiara could sense it—the undercurrent of jealousy, pain, and concern swirling beneath the surface of his words. She had known him long enough to understand that when his voice rose, it wasn't just anger—it was everything he had kept hidden for so long.

"Sameer… He's not what you think he is," he continued, his voice now cutting through the air, harsh and unyielding. "He's just trying to satisfy his own selfish desires. He's never going to leave his family for you. Do you really think he'll give up on everything for you? No. He wants the thrill of tasting fruit from a different tree, and once he's had his fill, he'll walk away. When you need him, when you're down, he won't be there. And when you're crying, he'll have excuses. You really think he's going to be there for you forever?" Aniket's words hit her like a slap.

She stood still, her breath momentarily trapped in her throat. It felt as if someone had plunged a sword straight into her chest. She had never seen him like this before—this was not the same soft-spoken, patient friend who had stood by her all these years. His words were harsh, cutting deeper than she could have imagined. His anger and concern were so palpable, so raw, and yet, she couldn't help but feel the sting of betrayal in them. How could he speak like this to her? She stared at him in disbelief, her heart shattering at the realization that this conversation was breaking something inside both.

"No, this can't be true," she whispered, her voice trembling. "Sameer would never hurt me. He'll never do that." She longed to believe it—she needed to believe it. She had convinced herself that Sameer was different, that he was the one who would never leave her, that he was the one who cared.

But Aniket wasn't done. He stepped closer, his hands gripping her shoulders with a force that startled her. His eyes bore into hers, filled with pain, frustration, and an undeniable desperation. "Mark my words, Kiara," he said, his voice low but firm. "He's going to make your life hell. You're nothing but a use-and-throw object to him. And when the time comes, he won't even look back. He'll walk away without a second thought, and you'll be left picking up the pieces. But here's the thing, Kiara... deep down, you know it. You know this is true. Why are you in denial? Why don't you ask yourself, really, what's going on here? You're afraid to face the truth, aren't you?"

His grip tightened on her shoulders as his words pierced through her defences. Kiara flinched, her breath quickening, as his words cut deeper. She felt the heat of his anger, his fists clenched around her shoulders so tightly that it hurt, and yet, there was a part of her that wanted to push him away—away from this truth she didn't want to face. Unable to bear the tension any longer, Kiara jerked her shoulders away from him, her eyes filled with despair. She couldn't look at him, couldn't face the depth of his words, because, in some part of her heart, she knew he was right. But she couldn't admit it—not to herself, not to him. She turned her face away, the weight of his words sinking in. "I don't know what to do anymore," she whispered, her voice barely audible against the hum of the city around them. "I don't know who to trust." And as the tears welled up again, she felt a part of her slipping away torn between the man who had always been there for her and the illusion of love that had consumed her heart for so long.

"I thought of all people, you would understand my pain," her voice trembled, thick with emotion. "At least you would be here with me during this time of complete uncertainty." You were my last hope of help!" Her words, laced with desperation, hung in the air, but instead of the comfort she had hoped for, she was met with a response that cut deeper than she could have imagined.

"Are you nuts?" he shot back, his voice rising with frustration. "You never recognized or appreciated my love for you, and now, you have the guts to talk about your distressed love life with a married man to me and expect me to empathize with you! What do you think of me? Am I a moron, a loser?" She hadn't expected this response, but as he spoke, it was clear that years of suppressed feelings were being unleashed. Without another word, he stood up abruptly and walked away. She was paralyzed, too stunned to move, her throat tight with grief. She couldn't summon the strength to call him back, to stop him. Her world felt like it was crumbling, and all she could do was sit there, lost in the silence, unable to process the whirlwind of emotions that had just erupted. Fifteen minutes passed in agonizing stillness before he returned. His face was unreadable, a mask of cold indifference.

"I think we're done," he said flatly.

"We should head home."

His words were final, a harsh declaration of their fractured reality. Without a word, Kiara rose mechanically to her feet, her body moving on autopilot. She followed him, each step feeling heavier than the last. They walked in silence toward the metro station, side by side but worlds apart. Though they were physically near, there was an ocean of distance between their souls, an unbridgeable gap that had formed in mere moments. She glanced up at him, her heart aching, and reached out instinctively to hold his hand, but he shrugged it off without a glance. His face was a stone mask—unemotional, uncaring. He was a stranger to her in that moment, and it felt as though the warmth they once shared had turned to ice. The ride on the train was filled with suffocating silence. No words. No glances. When they arrived at their respective destinations, there was no goodbye. No "See you soon." There was nothing. It was as if the bond they had shared for so many years had been irreparably broken, and now, it felt like the final chapter had been written. Later, as she sat in the quiet of her own room, her mind replayed everything Aniket had said. Deep down, she knew he was right, but the harshness of his words still stung. His version of the truth was too painful, too real for her to face. Her heart and mind were at odds, caught in a tug-of-war between what she knew and what she refused to accept. She didn't want to come out of the bubble she had created around herself, even though she knew it would eventually burst. She was fully aware that the world she had built was a fragile illusion, but she wasn't ready to let go of it yet. She was in complete denial, clinging to a fantasy that offered her comfort, even if it was fleeting. The truth loomed large in the distance, but she wasn't ready to face it—not yet.

> "*Love may deceive us, blind us, but a true friend will always find the courage to tell us what we need to hear, not what we want to hear.*"
>
> – *Unknown*

Gurgaon, 2011

In the Wake of Forbidden Love

The next day, Kiara walked into her workplace, feeling a mix of excitement and nervousness. As soon as she entered the floor, the entire team stood up and erupted into applause, whistling and cheering with broad smiles. "Welcome back!" they shouted in unison. She couldn't help but feel overwhelmed with joy, her face lighting up as she smiled warmly at her colleagues. "Thank you!" she replied, her heart swelling with gratitude. Everyone gathered around her to congratulate her on the successful project completion, offering hugs, handshakes, and words of praise. But amidst the congratulations, there was one person who stood apart—a colleague she had once felt a connection with. Initially, she had reached out to him for help during the project, thinking he was someone she could rely on. However, her perception of him had changed drastically when he had refused to assist her while she was in Chennai. To make matters worse, he had gone as far as to say, "This is what happens when you send immature and unprepared kids for critical projects. She'll fail and get kicked out." The bitterness of his words still lingered in her mind, but she pushed it aside as the team continued to celebrate. The room buzzed with excitement as everyone wanted to hear about her experience in Chennai—the South Indian food, the culture, the beautiful beaches, and just a little about the work. She was happy to share, and the conversation flowed effortlessly, filled with laughter and stories. For a moment, everything felt light, and she allowed herself to bask in the success of the project and the warmth of her colleagues' support. After the celebration died down, she settled into her desk to catch up on emails, something caught her eye. She saw a message from Sameer on G-Talk; it was short, but it stung: "Don't message me anymore here."

A wave of anxiety washed over her. The sudden coldness of his words left her feeling unsettled and desperate to reach out to him. She unlocked her phone, her fingers hovering over his contact, ready to call him. But the thought of his family quickly halted her. The guilt of his commitment to his wife and kids clawed at her, and she hesitated, the phone still in her trembling hand. Her mind raced, full of confusion and longing. Then, a sudden realization struck her. He must be in Chennai—he was supposed to fly back from Mumbai a day before. With renewed urgency, she dialled his number, but it rang and rang with no answer. Panic crept in as she wondered why he wouldn't pick up. She put her phone down, trying to calm her racing thoughts, but her curiosity got the better of her. She unlocked the screen and began casually scrolling through social media, hoping for some distraction. That's when she saw a new message from him.

It was brief but left her even more confused. "Don't call or message me. I'm still at home. I'll call back soon."

Her heart sank as she read the words. Something didn't feel right. Why was he still at home? And why had he been so distant? The message only added to her growing confusion and worry. What was going on with him? What did all this mean?

Her thoughts spiralled as she tried to make sense of it. The questions and doubt ate at her, yet she couldn't shake the sense that something was off. Was Sameer pulling away from her for good? Or was this just another twist in a complicated, confusing situation?

"Hey, join us for breakfast today, my mom made something special for all of us," one of her colleagues invited, a warm smile on his face. She instantly concocted an excuse to avoid the invitation. She wasn't in the mood for socializing, not when her mind was clouded by confusion and unspoken words. To distract herself, she buried herself in work, but it was easier said than done. No matter how much she tried to focus, her thoughts kept drifting back to him. He was the one she thought of with every breath, the one she couldn't shake off, no matter how hard she tried. She glanced at the clock, realizing how quickly the time had passed. "The hands move so fast. It's already lunchtime." Her team asked her again to join them, but she found another excuse, not wanting to face the world just yet. This time, Rehan noticed her withdrawn demeanour. He didn't say anything but the way he looked at her made it clear that he sensed something was bothering her. He sat at the desk opposite hers and didn't join the team for lunch either. She finished up the presentation she had been working on, her thoughts still tangled in a mess of emotions. She decided to go for lunch alone, needing some space to think, to clear her mind. But just as she was about to leave, Rehan looked up from his laptop and asked, "Can you wait for two minutes? I'll join you." She hesitated, yearning for some time alone, but she couldn't bring herself to say no to him. She waited, quietly grateful for the distraction. As they walked towards the cafeteria, chatting casually about office life, she found herself laughing at the silly emails clients often sent. For a moment, she was able to forget her worries and just enjoy the conversation. But then, as they rounded the corner, they spotted their team coming from the opposite direction. The team looked at them, exchanged mischievous glances, and teased, "Oh, you two wanted to go separately and spend some nice time together, huh?"

She rolled her eyes but managed to smile back, though inside, she felt irritated by the false impression. Rehan, on the other hand, was blushing, and she couldn't help but notice how awkward it made her feel. He turned to her, a concerned expression on his face. "Are you okay?"

"Yeah, I'm fine," she replied, her voice betraying the emotions swirling inside her.

"Let's go to the terrace. The weather's pleasant today. Not too sunny, not too gloomy, don't you think?" Rehan suggested, eager to get some fresh air.

She nodded, trying to shake off the discomfort. "Yeah, sure. You're right. Let's get some relief from this canned air."

They made their way to the terrace, finding a quiet corner table with two chairs. The breeze was soothing, a welcome change from the office's sterile atmosphere. As they sat down, Rehan broke the silence.

"I'm seeing you after a long time, superwoman! And I can't tell you how happy I am, but I don't see that happiness reciprocating. Is something bothering you?"

She tried to push her worries aside as she took a bite of her food, forcing a smile.

"There's nothing. It's just that I wanted to relax after the hectic project, but I had to come to work, so... I'm a little irritated."

He studied her for a moment, his gaze unwavering, but he seemed satisfied with her answer, not pressing her further. He knew something was off, but he didn't want to push her.

As they ate, he casually began sharing what had been happening in her absence.

"Most people here thought you were incapable and undeserving of the project. They didn't think you could finish it. There were a lot of negative comments, a lot of bad energy. Most people didn't say anything in front of me because of the perceived closeness between us, but you... you blew all that criticism away with your stellar performance."

Kiara chuckled, the compliment warming her heart. "Well, what can I say, Rehan? If a dog barks, you don't bark back!" Both laughed, feeling a brief sense of relief as the tension between them eased.

For a moment, she was able to just be herself, surrounded by the light-hearted banter and the comforting presence of a friend. It was a brief escape from the turmoil of her heart, a moment where the world didn't feel so heavy. But deep down, she knew she wasn't truly free from her thoughts. Sameer's message still lingered in her mind, and the questions about her future, her feelings, and her choices remained unanswered. By the time, both finished lunch and returned to their workstations, an issue came up. One of their colleagues, a fellow trainee who had joined around the same time as them, was being trained to handling an emergency issue and a live customer complaint. Both Kiara and Rehan were pulled in to help. For her, this was a new experience, one that felt overwhelming. It was as though she was drowning in a sea of tasks, her colleagues unable to throw her a lifeline. The customer complaints kept coming in, each one more urgent than the last. She was flustered, unsure where to begin in such a vast mess. Her hands trembled as she worked on the live system, each click feeling like a step into an unknown abyss. After thirty minutes of intense focus later, Rehan finally pinpointed the issue, and both quickly fixed it. The feeling of relief that washed over her was brief but satisfying. She had conquered yet another challenge.

She glanced at her watch absentmindedly. 3:30 p.m. Time had slipped away so quickly. The stress of both work and her complicated emotions were beginning to take a physical toll on her. Her stomach churned uncomfortably, and she thought to herself, "If my chums start now, I'll be as dead as a log. I better go back to the PG and sleep."

She approached Arjun, her manager, feeling faint and weak. "I'm not feeling well. Can I leave early today?" she asked.

Arjun looked up from his laptop, his concern immediately visible. He studied her pale face and immediately knew she wasn't faking it.

"Are you okay? Do you want me to drop you home?" he asked, his voice laced with genuine care.

Kiara shook her head. "No, I'll take the office cab. I just need some rest."

"Alright," Arjun said. "Call me if you need anything."

She smiled faintly at him, grateful for his understanding, and left his cabin.

As she walked away, Arjun couldn't help but think to himself, "Such a powerhouse of activity packed into such a small body. Big things come in small packages. We're lucky to have hired her."

Kiara packed her things quickly, not wanting to linger in the office any longer. She headed straight to the elevator without looking at anyone, avoiding any further interactions. Instead of waiting for the office cab, she took an auto-rickshaw, eager to get back to her PG. Once she arrived, she went straight to her room and collapsed into bed, hoping the sleep would numb her thoughts, even if just for a little while. She closed her eyes, hoping to escape the emotional storm swirling within her. When she woke up later that evening, the clock read 6:30 p.m. She slowly sat up, rubbing her eyes, and reached for her phone. She scrolled through her messages, her call log—anything to see if Sameer had responded. But there was nothing. No call, no message. Just an empty screen. Disappointment washed over her, but she fought back the tears. The ache in her heart was familiar, but this time, it felt different—more suffocating, more unbearable. Despite the painful life she'd lived, the weight of this sorrow felt impossible to carry. The absence of his words, the silence between them, cut deeper than she had imagined. She sat there, her thoughts swirling, trying to piece together what had gone wrong. Why hasn't he called? she kept asking herself. Have I done something wrong? All these questions took over her mind. As she retraced her steps, she realized the gravity of her actions. She had been caught up in the whirlwind of emotions, but now, reflecting on it, she understood the consequences. She was hurting people, and the weight of that guilt was heavy on her heart.

Her conscience was loud and clear, urging her to do the right thing. She decided: the next day, she would call Sameer and tell him that whatever was happening between them wasn't right. They needed to maintain distance for the sake of everyone involved. It was the only way to stop the situation from spiralling further. Just as she was formulating the words she would say to him, her phone screen lit up, and his name flashed across. Do things ever go as planned? she wondered. She picked up the phone, her breath catching in her throat as soon as he uttered the word "Baby." Everything she had decided to say evaporated. Instead of confronting him, she found herself asking about his whereabouts and expressing how much she missed him. He apologized for not calling sooner and reassured her, "Baby, listen to me, I don't have much time. I just stepped out to buy something from a nearby store, and I'm calling you from here." His voice sounded rushed, as if the weight of the situation was bearing down on him.

He continued, "When I was packing my stuff on Sunday, my wife came across our messages. She caught me. I was in such a bad situation—I felt like my life was falling apart in pieces. I convinced her, for now, that I wouldn't keep in touch with you, but don't worry. I'll find a solution soon. I've made promises to you too." His words painted a grim picture."

"I had to call a few friends in Chennai to help me convince my wife. One of them was Shalini, the one from whose house we had the late-night Paani puri," he continued. Kiara was taken aback by the mention of Shalini and her surprise act.

"Because of all this, I had to cancel my travel plans. I'll be heading to Chennai tomorrow instead. I even spoke to the guesthouse staff on speakerphone in front of my wife, just to assure her that you had already left Chennai."

There was a long pause before he asked, "Won't you say anything?"

"You may be running late, but before you go, I want to remind you that you can't always have everything."

Sameer sounded surprised, almost confused. "What does that mean?" he asked, his voice blending curiosity with a hint of disbelief.

She stayed silent, unsure how to explain herself. Her words had come from a place of frustration, and now, she wasn't sure she had the strength to continue the conversation.

Sameer seemed to sense her hesitation. "I must leave, but I need to know what that means. So, please be prepared for the next call."

After the call ended, she kept on staring at her phone. The heaviness in her chest was almost unbearable. In our next conversation, she thought, "I must end this fling."

The guilt that had been building up inside her for days now seemed unbearable, like a weight she couldn't lift. She felt nauseous, not just physically, but emotionally, as the full scope of her actions started to sink in. What have I done? she wondered, the guilt gnawing at her. It wasn't just about the affair—it was about the lives she was impacting, the people she was hurting. She knew she couldn't keep going down this path, but she also didn't know how to stop.

The next day began like any other, with Kiara going through the same monotonous routine. But this time, there was an underlying sadness that weighed heavily on her. She had lost her one and only childhood friend, Aniket, all because of her feelings for Sameer. It felt like a double-edged sword, wounding her from both sides. Aniket and Kiara hadn't spoken since their last encounter at India Gate. She had tried calling him several times, but each time, her calls went unanswered. Aniket's heartbreak was a barrier that he could not cross, and it hurt Kiara more than she had ever anticipated.

That day, Sameer was traveling back to Chennai, and she couldn't shake the feeling that he would call her. She had mixed emotions—part of her wanted to talk to him, but another part of her knew the conversation would bring her even closer to the uncomfortable truth she had been avoiding.

As she made her way through the office reception, greeting her colleagues, her phone buzzed. She glanced at the screen and saw Sameer's name. A smile involuntarily crept onto her face, but it was short-lived as the weight of everything hit her. She felt detached from everything around her, like she was in her own world—silent, muted.

"Hello?" she answered, her voice barely above a whisper.

Sameer's familiar husky voice greeted her on the other end, "I reached Chennai. Do you have some time to talk?"

"Okay, but before you start talking, give me a minute. Let me find a quiet place where we can talk peacefully."

She walked toward an empty meeting room and closed the door behind her. She sat in silence, staring out the large glass windows at the vast expanse of steel and glass structures. The view was cold and impersonal, just like the emptiness she felt inside. She was expecting a conversation, but what Sameer was about to share wasn't a conversation at all—it was a monologue that shattered everything. He began without any pleasantries, his words tumbling out.

"The other day, I told my wife that I met you in Chennai, and I'm friends with you. She was cool about it, but later in the evening, while I was packing my stuff, she scanned my email account and phone. She read all the messages exchanged between you and me. After reading the conversations, she completely broke down. She was howling and crying."

Kiara's heart raced as he kept talking. "I asked her, 'What's wrong? Why are you crying?' She demanded to know, 'Who the hell is Kiara, and what's going on between you and me?'

I said her, "You are just a friend."

At that moment, everything stopped for Kiara. The words "just a friend" landed on her like a heavy blow. The world around her seemed to blur as she became momentarily deaf to everything he said after that. The sound of his voice, the noise of the office, the world outside—it all faded away. She could barely process what he was saying. Just a friend? Was that all she was to him? After everything—the late-night conversations, the emotions, the promises—he had reduced her to nothing more than a friend? Tears began to roll down her cheeks, and before she could stop herself, she interrupted him, her voice trembling, "Am I nothing else to you other than just a friend?"

Her words hung in the air, heavy and heartbreaking. She felt an overwhelming rush of emotions—betrayal, confusion, and a deep sense of worthlessness. He had never truly acknowledged the depth of what they shared. To him, it was a fleeting connection, something insignificant that he could easily dismiss. The silence that followed was deafening. She could barely hear the faint sound of his voice trying to explain, but she was too broken to listen. It was as if her entire world had shattered in that one moment. She had hoped, foolishly perhaps, that there was more to their bond than what he was willing to admit, but now it felt like it was all a lie.

His voice came through the phone again, but this time it was distant and hollow. "Kiara… I… I didn't mean it like that. I never wanted to hurt you. I just—"

But she couldn't take it anymore. She ended the call, her heart shattered into a thousand pieces. She had never felt more alone, more lost, or more betrayed in her life.

Few seconds later, her phone buzzed again.

His voice, full of frustration and pleading, echoed through Kiara's ears, but she was resolute. "It's not like that, baby! To convince my wife, I said so; but I didn't mean it. I had no other option. I've kids, and I cannot leave them. The way I love you, I love them too."

She absorbed his words, feeling a profound sadness settle over her. She knew, deep down, that this was a lie. He was torn between two worlds, but the truth was undeniable: he could never have both. It's a gut wrenching feeling to share the love of your life with someone else. Her heart ached, but she gathered the courage to speak, her voice steady but filled with sorrow.

"Do you remember what I told you last time? You can't always have it all. It means that you can't be with me and your family. You have to make choices, stand by them, and prioritize things—even if you're not happy."

His tone was defensive, his stress bubbling over.

"Baby, I'm already stressed out. Don't make this harder for me."

His words stung, but Kiara understood. He was drowning in his conflicting emotions, unable to make sense of the situation. Yet, despite everything, she pressed on.

"When you didn't speak to me for so long, I realized that I'm the one who's ruining several lives. I'm not doing the right thing. Because of me, you aren't faithful to the woman who has been beside you for the past six years—who is the mother of your children. And you can never be mine."

He raised his voice, defensively, "Who is saying that I'm not yours? I'm yours and you are mine, but I've certain responsibilities toward my family too."

Kiara, feeling the weight of his words, snapped back. "See? Who's talking about responsibility now?

Being honest with your family is the most important thing, don't you think? Have our ethics flown out of the window?"

For a moment, there was silence. Then, after a brief pause, he muttered, "Baby, I think you're in a mood to push me over the edge." She could almost feel the frustration radiating from him, his clenched teeth and arched brows. But she wasn't going to back down. Her decision had already been made. She clarified, her voice quiet but firm. "No, you're taking it the wrong way. I'm just saying that our relationship has no future. We need to stop talking. It would be better for both of us to end this and stop running away from our real selves. Let's leave each other before the love leaves us."

"I don't understand what you're talking about."

"Okay. Call me back when you're in a stable state of mind and want to discuss this further," said her.

With a heavy heart, she ended the call. She felt a mix of anger and sadness, but beneath it all, there was a strange sense of satisfaction. For the first time in a long while, she felt in control of her life, control of the situation. She had made the hard decision to walk away. Returning to her desk, she tried to focus on the mountain of work before her, but it was impossible. Her mind kept drifting back to the conversation, to the guilt, and to the painful realization that everything she had been chasing was nothing but an illusion. Her colleagues noticed the change in her, but none of them dared to ask. They could see the sadness in her eyes, the weight she carried in her posture, but no one knew how to help. She was trapped in her own mind, struggling between the temptation of instant gratification and the pull of her moral compass. We often know what we are doing is morally wrong, but we still pursue it because it gives us instant happiness. The sense of euphoria rots the roots of morality.

She had experienced the momentary thrill, the fleeting happiness of a forbidden love, but now she was paying the price. The weight of her choices was sinking in, and the consequences of her actions loomed large.

> “*It's hard to wait around for something you know might never happen, but it's even harder to give up when you know it's everything you want.*”
>
> – *Unknown*

Gurgaon, 2011

The Truth Between Us

For the next few days, there was complete silence. The Casanova and his muse had fallen off the radar. Kiara found herself missing his voice, her heart aching with the kind of pain that made her feel as though someone had kicked her in the gut. She longed for his presence, for the comfort of his words, but the silence seemed endless. Days passed, then weeks. She learned to wear her smile like a mask, perfected the art of hiding the pain, and buried the tears that wanted to surface. True love, she realized, was a tough teacher. The pain of parting wasn't easy to swallow, but life had a way of moving forward, even when your heart was left behind. She did her best to move on, trying to mend the wounds and repair the cracks in her heart. But despite her best efforts, she couldn't forget him. And just when she thought she was finding peace, her phone buzzed on a sunny morning, breaking the stillness. It was him.

Waking up to his call, she answered the phone with a simple, "Hello."

"Baby am I audible to you?" his voice came through, smooth and familiar, yet distant.

"Yes. I can hear you."

"When will you be free from work today?"

"Around 5 p.m." she responded, unsure of where this conversation was heading.

"Well, in that case, you need to leave early today. I'm on my way to Gurgaon from Mumbai."

For a moment, Kiara froze. The words didn't register at first, and her mind scrambled to make sense of it. "When did you plan this? Why didn't you inform me? What about what we discussed the other day? Have you forgotten everything?"

His tone shifted, a touch more urgent, "For now, please don't ask me anything. Don't give me any lectures. We'll talk when we meet. I'm heading to the airport now. I'll call you once I've checked in."

Her heart skipped a beat, a mixture of surprise and elation flooding her. But she quickly masked her excitement. She wanted to stay firm, keep her resolve, no matter how much her heart yearned for him.

"Met a friend at the airport. I'll call you once I reach Gurgaon," messaged Sameer.

Kiara quickly did the math in her head. He would be arriving in Gurgaon around 3:00 p.m. He had asked her to book a room for them. She managed to secure a room in a nice 4-star hotel near the airport. It costs a fortune, especially in a city like Gurgaon, but she didn't mind. She was so used to her dreary, predictable life, and now, suddenly, everything seemed to be changing. The world she knew, once coloured in shades of Gray, was suddenly bursting with color. Life was chaotic, thrilling, and unpredictable once again. And yet, she couldn't shake the feeling that this whirlwind of emotions was just another facet of the dichotomy of life—how joy and pain often collided in the most unexpected of ways. Soon after lunch, Kiara's manager called for a team meeting. As she settled into her seat, Rehan leaned over and whispered, "I'm happy for you today. You've been so gloomy these past few days, but today, you seem re-energized. It's good to see you like this."

She was taken aback as she hadn't expected Rehan to notice, much less comment on it.

"Are you hiding something?"

"No," she replied, with a casual air, hiding the whirlwind of emotions inside her.

Just as the meeting was about to begin, her phone buzzed. She glanced down and saw the familiar name flashing across the screen. "Baby, I've reached; see you in another 20 minutes."

Surprised, Kiara muttered to herself, "What?! How come so early?" She quickly responded, "I've booked a room near the airport, but I've got an important meeting now. I'll take some time to come. Can you please come to my office and wait in the food court instead?"

"Well, Ok. In that case, how about the booking?"

"I'll cancel it and book somewhere near the office. Don't worry about it."

She quickly disconnected the call and shared her location with him. While her colleagues speculated about the impromptu meeting's agenda, she was lost in a whirlwind of thoughts, still trying to process the surprise he had sprung on her.

"Sometimes, meeting a loved one can be so stressful," she thought to herself.

In the middle of the meeting, her phone buzzed again.

"This guy is so impatient!" she thought, feeling a rush of frustration. She disconnected the call, quickly trying to focus on the presentation Arjun was giving. The PowerPoint slides were filled with complex charts and diagrams. Her eyes scanned the slides, but nothing registered.

"I've reached; I'm standing in front of the building," Sameer's message read.

"Please wait in the food court. It will take me a little longer."

As the meeting ran past its allotted time, she felt her impatience grow. She excused herself from the room, telling Arjun she had a personal emergency.

"Are you feeling alright?" Arjun asked, concerned.

"I'll be back in a minute. Just need to step out."

"Okay, sure. Go ahead," Arjun said, returning to the presentation.

She made a swift exit, heading straight for the food court. Her heart raced, but she couldn't help but feel a strange mix of excitement and anxiety. There was a lot to juggle, but right now, seeing Sameer felt like it was the only thing that mattered. She couldn't help but stare at him. The moment their eyes met, everything else seemed to fade away. There he was. The same man who had once made her heart race with the simplest of glances, now standing before her in the flesh, looking even more irresistible than she remembered. His hair, a little unkempt as if he'd just gotten out of bed, gave him that effortlessly cool vibe. The aviators perched on his nose only added to the mystery, and the sleek leather sling bag slung over his shoulder made him look like he had just stepped out of a fashion magazine. His navy-blue polo t-shirt, casually tucked into beige loose trousers, complimented his broad shoulders, while his blue tennis shoes added a touch of laid-back charm to his overall look. She felt a sudden rush of adrenaline surge through her body. The world around them seemed to stop, the bustling office space fading into a blur. All she could hear was the thumping of her own heartbeat as the spark between them reignited. It was the kind of connection that was impossible to describe, the kind that made her feel as if she'd known him forever. The kind that made her want to hug him, kiss him, and never let go. But there was no time for that. Not here, not now. They were in a public space, and both knew the importance of keeping their composure. With a soft smile, she quickly regained her balance, the slight wobble in her step betraying her flustered state. "I just came to see you," her voice warm. "But the meeting is still ongoing. I'll finish up and come back in a while. Meanwhile, you can have lunch."

"Really? I travelled 2,000 kilometres just to see you, and now I have to eat alone?" he teased, glancing at the bustling office kitchen in the distance.

He gave her an exaggerated puppy face, his eyes wide with mock sadness. "Tragic, right?" he said, his tone dripping with playful sarcasm.

Kiara couldn't help but laugh, shaking her head. "Well, that's what happens when you give surprises."

"Darling," he said, his smile widening as he leaned in slightly, "I saw that coming."

The laughter between them was light, easy. The kind of laughter that only people who truly understood each other could share. There was no need for words to fill the silence; their bond was palpable in the air between them. She could feel the warmth spreading through her chest, a mix of happiness and contentment. She wanted nothing more than to just leave everything behind and spend the day with him, but duty called. The meeting was important.

"Fine," he said, still smiling, "I'll let you off the hook for now. But you owe me a proper lunch when I'm free."

She rolled her eyes, her heart swelling with affection. "Okay, okay. I'll make it up to you later, I promise."

He gave her a cheeky grin. "See you in a bit, then. I'll be waiting for you."

As Kiara turned to head back into the meeting room, she caught Sameer's gaze one last time. The spark was still there, as intense as ever, and it made her chest tighten with the realization that this man, this connection, was her greatest adventure. With a smile, she pushed the door open and returned to her colleagues, her thoughts already wandering to when she'd see him again. The meeting had finally wrapped up around 2:15 p.m., and Kiara wasted no time informing Arjun that she'd be leaving for the day due to some personal errands. She grabbed her bag and hurried back to the food court, excitement building with each step as she thought about the rest of the day with Sameer. When she reached the bustling café, she found him already waiting for her at a table. The comfy cushioned chairs provided the perfect spot to relax, and his playful gaze as she sat down made her smile. He leaned back, raising an eyebrow, and said with a hint of sarcasm, "Shall we plan the evening together or spend it here only?"

She glanced around, taking in the lively atmosphere, the aroma of fresh coffee wafting through the air.

"This is a good enough place, with decent food, great coffee, and good service!" she replied with a smirk.

"Baby, you've also learnt the art of sarcasm," he teased.

"You taught me well."

Her gaze shifted from him to her phone, her fingers tapping away on the screen as she looked up hotel options nearby. Sameer's playful expression faltered, and he gave her a disapproving look. "Stop playing with your phone, baby! Which hotel have you booked?"

With a mischievous glint in her eyes, she responded, "Not booked yet," while still scrolling through the booking app.

He let out a mock gasp, his voice dripping with disbelief. "Seriously?" He mumbled something under his breath, shaking his head in mock exasperation.

Kiara, undeterred, finally secured a room at a nearby hotel. "Let's go! We're all set!" she declared triumphantly.

"I can't believe you. Let's go."

They decided to walk to the hotel instead of taking a cab. Walking together had always been something they enjoyed, especially when they were in Chennai, where they'd shared so many quiet strolls and deep conversations. They talked about everything and nothing—work, health, food, the latest TV show they'd watched. It felt easy and familiar, like nothing had changed between them, even though so much had. When they finally reached the hotel lobby, they were greeted by a receptionist who asked for their IDs and their relationship. Kiara glanced at Sameer, who looked at her with a soft smile before answering, "She's, my fiancée." A wave of warmth spread through her chest. She didn't let the smile that tugged at her lips grow too wide, though, not wanting to make a scene. Still, hearing him say those words felt like a quiet affirmation of everything she had ever hoped for. The receptionist, surprised but clearly pleased, nodded and handed them their room key. A hotel staff member came to escort them to their room. As they entered the lift, he turned to the female staff and gestured, "After you, ma'am," with a charming smile. Her heart fluttered. She valued those small, chivalrous gestures more than she could explain, and his thoughtfulness made her smile wider. It was one of the many things that made him so special in her eyes. As the lift doors closed and they ascended to their floor, she leaned against him, her heart full of anticipation for what the rest of the day would bring.

Upon entering the room, she was momentarily lost for words. The décor was nothing short of breathtaking. It wasn't just beautiful; it felt like stepping into a dream. The space was expansive, the warmth of the wooden panelling wrapping around her like a comforting embrace. The pearl-white bedsheet was perfectly smooth, almost inviting her to fall onto it. The contemporary furniture, sleek and minimalist, stood elegantly against the backdrop of the warm wooden walls. Hemmed double-layered curtains framed the windows, their soft fabric rippling slightly in the gentle breeze that seeped through. The TV, tucked discreetly into one corner, emitted a soft ambient light, adding to the serene atmosphere. What took her breath away the most, however, was the lighting. There was no visible source of light, except for the soft glow of a chandelier that hung gracefully from the ceiling, casting a dreamy aura across the room. The large floor tiles reflected the light just enough to create an inviting, smooth surface that felt cool beneath her feet. In certain sections, a soft, plush carpet awaited her steps, making her feet feel as though they were sinking into something luxurious. The soft blue hues emanated from nowhere—just the kind of mysterious touch that made the room feel otherworldly. The gentle floral aroma that filled the air was intoxicating, as if the room itself had a soul. She stood there, her mind trying to absorb the magnificence of it all. She was befuddled by the beauty.

Sameer's gentle tap on her shoulder bought her back to the present moment.

With a wink, she shot him a playful look before rushing to the bathroom. The moment she stepped inside, her breath caught in her throat. A full-sized tub, big enough to drown her worries, stood proudly in the middle of the room, surrounded by an elegant set of herbal toiletries. White towels with "His" and "Hers" embroidered in delicate letters were neatly arranged. The sink, like everything else in the room, was spotless and enormous—so much so that she briefly wondered if she could fit in it herself! She smiled at the absurd thought. This was everything she had ever dreamed of; a life that seemed so far away when she was a child. As she stared at her reflection in the mirror, her inner conscience posed a question that tugged at her heart: "Is life complete without true love?" The thought threatened to unravel the happiness she had worked so hard to build. She pushed it aside, trying to ignore the gnawing feeling that had crept into her mind. With a deep breath, she walked toward the balcony, hoping the view would distract her. The room was on the 14th floor, and as she stepped outside, she was engulfed by the mesmerizing sight before her. The city sprawled out below her, a blend of concrete and greenery, bustling with life. The sun had started to dip lower in the sky, casting an amber glow across the horizon. Kiara was lost in the moment, the beauty of it all washing over her, when she felt a presence behind her. Before she could react, Sameer's arms wrapped around her waist, pulling her close. The sensation was gentle, but it sent a rush of emotions through her. His touch, after so long, was like a balm to her soul. The warmth of his arms around her, the steady beat of his heart against her back, brought tears to her eyes. Tears of joy. Not sadness, but joy—a joy she hadn't known she could feel until this moment. She turned in his embrace and looked up at him, her heart bursting with love. Without a word, she wrapped her arms around his neck and hugged him tightly. He cupped her face with his hands, his touch tender as he kissed her forehead. As he pulled back slightly, his gaze softened. Kiara could feel the weight of her own insecurities creeping in. The fear of losing him—the only man who had ever truly loved her—gripped her heart tightly. She had always been fearless when she had nothing to lose, but now, with everything she had ever wanted within reach, the fear of losing it all made her terrified of the very idea of fear itself. Without thinking twice, Kiara buried her face in his chest, seeking comfort, a refuge from the overwhelming emotions she couldn't fully understand. Sameer's face rested on the top of her head; his arms wrapped around her protectively. They stood there, close yet distant, their hearts communicating more than words ever could. But even as they stood together, the thought lingered in the back of her mind: Could they ever truly be together in the way she dreamed?

In the absence of certainty, she found herself clinging to the warmth of his embrace, hoping that this moment, this connection, could last forever. They stood there for what felt like an eternity, their hearts beating in sync, both lost in the gravity of the moment. The world around them seemed to disappear, leaving only the two of them, locked in an embrace that was both comforting and full of longing.

Sameer finally broke the silence, his voice a soft murmur against her hair. "I never gave up on you. I remembered you each night. You don't know how much I missed you in the three weeks when we didn't speak. I kept checking my phone every minute, hoping for your message."

Kiara lifted her head slowly, their gazes meeting once again. She could see the raw emotion in his eyes—the same longing she had buried in her own heart. He tightened his grip around her, pulling her closer. "Though it's not very saintly to have an extramarital affair, logic and reasoning aren't getting processed in my heart that my brain is trying to enforce upon," he admitted, his words laced with vulnerability.

She held his gaze, her heart both aching and fluttering. She had always believed in logic, in the right path, in the rules. But in this moment, she felt something deeper—something beyond reason.

His voice was thick with emotion as he continued, "I want to be with you forever. God is putting me at the crossroads of a dangerous juncture in life. I wish things could have been straightforward, but they aren't. Let's enjoy this moment; let's live every moment like it's our last."

Kiara never agreed with the ideology of "living each day as if it's your last." She was a planner, someone who believed in mapping out her future with careful thought and precision. She would plan for days, even weeks ahead for anything, making sure there were no surprises or uncertainties. But as Sameer's words lingered in the air, she began to wonder if there was some truth to it.

God, it seemed, had a funny way of imposing beliefs on those who didn't believe in them.

"I have my flight tomorrow evening," he said softly. "I want to make the most of these two days."

Her heart raced. She understood the urgency in his voice, the intensity of his words. He wanted to seize these final moments, to make every second count, to feel the depth of their connection in a way that would stay with them forever. She looked up at him. The weight of his words, the reality of their fleeting time together, overwhelmed her. She knew she couldn't stop the inevitable. Life, love, and time—they were all moving in their own directions, and no matter how much they tried to hold on, they were both bound by forces greater than them. Tears welled in her eyes, and without a word, she lifted her face toward him. Seeing the sadness and longing in her eyes, he couldn't resist any longer. His hand gently cupped her face, and without a second thought, he kissed her. It was their first kiss. Their lips met softly, tenderly, but as the kiss deepened, it became more urgent, more passionate—both pouring everything they had into that single, unforgettable moment. He connected his mobile to the Bluetooth speakers in the room, and the soft strains of "Pehli Nazar Mein" filled the air, wrapping the room in an intimate, romantic atmosphere. He glanced at her with a playful smile and asked, "Shall we dance?"

She smiled but shook her head, a hint of reluctance in her eyes. "No," she murmured.

But he wasn't one to give up easily. With a gentle pull, he drew her towards him. "Please?" he asked, his voice low and sincere.

She couldn't resist the tenderness in his eyes. The look in his eyes betrayed her thoughts. Before she knew it, their feet were moving in sync, the rhythm of the song guiding their every step. One of his hands held hers gently, while his other hand wrapped around her waist, pulling her closer, yet with such a tender embrace that it felt more like an invitation than a demand. The song, one of their favorites, played on, and the soft melody seemed to echo the emotions both were feeling. While they swayed together, he spoke again, his voice full of light-heartedness. "When we were in Chennai, you hinted that you loved dancing. So, when I got back to Mumbai, I enrolled myself and my wife in a dance class."

"Your wife?"

"Yeah, my wife was ecstatic about it. Little did she know why I had signed up. I don't know whether I should be happy or ashamed!"

They both smiled, lightening the moment, even if the underlying complexity of their situation loomed.

"I've been planning to surprise you with my dancing skills since we stopped talking."

Her smile faltered slightly as the weight of their unspoken words settled between them. "I'm sorry," she said, her voice quiet. "I never meant to hurt you, but our relationship wasn't going anywhere. I felt so… directionless. I couldn't concentrate on anything; the guilt and remorse were just… too much."

"I get it. I know what you were and are going through. We both have been sailing in the same rudderless ship," he said gently. "But let's not talk about this for the next two days, okay? I want to love you and be loved by you. I want to enjoy the little things with you here in Delhi."

He gently lifted her in his arms, surprising her with his strength. "I'm very heavy," she protested shyly, her voice tinged with embarrassment. "Please don't lift me."

"You're just 45 kilograms. I can't even feel your weight on my arms," he teased, his smirk full of affection.

A blush creeped across her cheeks. He laid her gently on the bed, the softness of the sheets adding to the intimacy of the moment. She continued to watch him with a mixture of curiosity and anticipation. Kneeling, he carefully removed her stilettos, placing them on the floor. Then, with a graceful movement, he removed his own shoes. He came closer, his presence enveloping her as he kissed her forehead, his lips warm against her skin. He took her hands in his, his fingers entwining with hers, before he lay down beside her, facing her. He tightened his grip on her hand, as if anchoring himself to the moment, and kissed her hand once more. The tenderness of the gesture, the softness of his touch, spoke volumes.

"What are we going to do now?" she asked softly, her voice laced with a hint of anticipation.

I've visited Delhi for the first time so that I want to do everything that you love, together."

She let out a laugh, the idea bringing a playful spark to her eyes. "If you want to visit all the places that I love, then we should probably get started now itself."

He leaned in, planting a gentle kiss on her cheek before getting up. "Alright, Darling. Time to get moving!"

As he went to freshen up, she quickly began mentally mapping out their itinerary. Red Fort, Chandani Chowk, Purana Qila, India Gate, and Connaught Place—these were the must-see landmarks she had in mind. When he returned from the bathroom, the room was filled with a subtle fragrance. Kiara, sensing it immediately, sprang out of bed and ran over to him. "Nice fragrance! It can be none other than BVLGARI," she said, grinning.

"You live in a PG, on a budget, and yet you know BVLGARI? That's so strange. What's the secret, baby?"

She burst into laughter at his surprise, loosening her grip on him before dashing off to the restroom to get ready. Sameer watched her go, amused.

A few minutes later, Kiara emerged, looking fresh-faced and glowing with her natural beauty. "Love your no-makeup look," he remarked.

"You don't like women with makeup, or you don't like me wearing makeup?"

"I don't like anyone wearing makeup. God made us all beautiful. Why hide it with all those cosmetics?"

Kiara smiled, impressed with his perspective. "Interesting," she said, bending down to put on her sneakers. But then, she froze—suddenly struggling with the laces. Knowing her well, he offered to help.

"Don't worry about the small stuff when I'm with you."

"What if one day, you're not around?" she asked, her voice quieter, filled with a mixture of vulnerability and uncertainty.

The question hung in the air, and for a moment, the room fell into a heavy silence. Neither of them spoke, unsure of how to answer. The only thing they could do was hold onto each other, tightly, as if the grip itself could prevent the fear from creeping in. Breaking the quiet, Kiara softly recited lines from her favourite poet, Nida Fazil, her voice low and contemplative.

> "*Kabhi kisi ko mukamal jahan nahi milta*
> *Kisi ko zameen kisi ko aasman nahi milta*
> *Tamam duniya me aisa nahi ki pyar nahi milta*
> *Jahan Umeed hoi iski bus wahan nahi milta*"
>
> *– Nida Fazil*

He listened intently, his heart aching with the weight of her words. He squeezed her hand, the silence between them now filled with a deeper understanding of their fears, their hopes, and the fleeting nature of their time together. The moment lingered before they finally broke away, each lost in thought, yet inexplicably closer than ever. They started their evening with a metro ride toward Rajiv Chowk. The train was packed, and there was hardly any room to stand. Sameer found a corner and gently pulled Kiara to him, holding her waist as the train swayed with the crowd. Kiara, feeling the warmth of his touch, loved the moment. Unlike most people who were impatiently waiting for a seat, she secretly hoped they wouldn't find one. Sometimes, isn't the journey more exciting than the destination, she thought. As they exited the metro, Sameer marvelled at how the Delhi government had managed to build such an underground system in the middle of a bustling street. They began walking toward a quieter lane lined with restaurants and luxury brand shops. After a short stroll, they found a small, unassuming restaurant, not too flashy but inviting, nonetheless. She smiled, recalling the saying, "Don't judge a book by its cover." This place embodied that sentiment perfectly.

Inside, the restaurant had a minimalist contemporary décor, with dimly lit table lamps that softened the space. The pink hue on the walls seemed to brighten the mood instantly, creating a cozy, intimate atmosphere. It was the perfect setting for a quiet dinner for two. They sat at a corner table in the balcony, surrounded by comfortable armchairs with soft pillows. The sound of the soft music played in the background combined with the bustling streets below, made the evening feel like a beautiful, private escape.

Sameer took the lead to order the food and as always, he was quick.

"We're pretty much sorted for today. We'll have food, listen to some nice music, and later, we'll head to India Gate for a peaceful walk."

"You're fast at making decisions and such a meticulous planner, though I'll never forget how you made me wait outside your office for nearly two hours."

She laughed softly, savouring the warmth of the moment. The evening, with its simple pleasures, felt just right.

"Here's your order. Hope you enjoy your meal," said the waiter.

The food arrived, piping hot and scrumptious. The waiter placed the dishes in front of them, and before they could dig in, the waiter informed them about a Karaoke and Salsa event happening that evening at the restaurant. With a glance, Sameer turned to her, his eyes asking if she was interested. She smiled and signalled a definite "yes." Without hesitation, they both enrolled for the event. As soon as they had completed the sign-up, she hesitated for a moment and said, "I'm no expert in dancing or singing at all."

"I already told you, when I'm around, you don't have to worry about anything. I'll take care of it." she nodded, feeling a sense of comfort and excitement.

They dug into the food, savouring every bite. The evening was still young, and the moment was perfect. After finishing their meal, they headed up to the rooftop where the event was already in full swing. The atmosphere was vibrant, with music from the golden era of Bollywood playing through—mostly songs from the 70s and 80s. Tracks by Kishore Kumar and R.D. Burman filled the air, both of whom were favorites of Sameer and Kiara. As they listened, they held hands, soaking in the nostalgia and joy of the moment, even though they weren't dancing yet. Soon enough, their names were announced for the Salsa and they both rushed to the dance floor. The Karaoke singer kicked off the performance with "Oh, Haseena Zulfon Wali," and both couldn't help but laugh. They danced, not as experts in Salsa, but with pure abandon—what could only be called "madly enjoying the moment." Their joy was infectious, and soon they were pulling a few other people from the crowd onto the floor. As the Karaoke singer switched to another classic, "Aajkal Tere Mere Pyar Ke Charche," the entire crowd seemed to be transported back to the late 60s. Everyone began tapping their feet and clapping along. The energy was contagious, and the night seemed to get even livelier.

Amidst the fun, Sameer pulled Kiara close, wrapping his arms around her, and kissed her. The crowd erupted into applause and cheers, and as they made their way away from stage, the moment felt perfect—pure, happy, and full of love. After the event, they decided to leave and take a peaceful walk toward India Gate, craving some quiet "us" time away from the excitement of the evening. The road was calm, the night sky clear, and the mild breeze made the walk even more serene. He glanced at her, but didn't say anything. She, too, caught his gaze for a moment but remained silent. The peace of the moment was enough.

They reached India Gate. The area around the gate was a sprawling garden, filled with life during the day, but now it was quieter.

Sameer tightened his grip on her hand as they strolled together.

"It's great to be roaming around this historic city with you. I couldn't have imagined it any other way."

"I thought you travel a lot for work. Don't you explore solo?"

"Well, I mostly travel for work, so I don't really get the chance to explore the rhythm and heartbeat of the cities. Traveling as a tourist, with someone you enjoy being with, is a whole different experience. Isn't it?"

"That's true," she said softly.

After a while, they decided to head back to the hotel. The night air had grown cooler, and she began to feel the chill. Sameer, ever thoughtful, slipped his jacket over her shoulders to keep her warm. They had already walked quite a bit and were already tired. Kiara quickly pulled out her phone and booked a cab, guiding the driver toward the India Gate entry point. Within moments, the cab arrived. Sameer opened the door for her, a gesture she appreciated deeply. As she climbed into the car, she smiled at him. He joined her from the other side, looking at her with affection. He leaned in and kissed her, wrapping his arms around her as she rested her head on his shoulder. She felt a sense of peace wash over her, and before she knew it, she had drifted off to sleep, completely relaxed in his embrace. This was the most peaceful sleep she had in last 3-4 weeks. When they arrived at the hotel, he gently rubbed her cheeks, waking her from her nap. She stirred, looking up at him, and found herself smiling at how beautiful and calm she felt.

As they entered their room, already exhausted, they fell immediately on the bed.

"This is so comfortable!"

He lay down beside her and started caressing her back, his touch tender and caring. She hugged him tightly, resting her head on his chest. She loved the feel of his skin, the warmth of his body, and, strangely, the comforting rhythm of his heartbeat. They both shared a quiet moment, their affection growing as they continued to be close. Their bond deepened, and as the hours passed, they took their intimacy to the next level, feeling more connected than ever before. The morning light came, bringing a fresh perspective. The sun's rays filtered through the hemmed curtains, casting playful patterns on Kiara's face. Sameer, watching her, couldn't help but admire her beauty. His rough yet gentle hands brushed her ruffled hair away from her face, his heart full of tenderness.

"She looks gorgeous," he thought, feeling an overwhelming sense of awe. In that moment, she seemed like an angel, so perfect and serene that he was almost afraid to touch her. But as he looked at her, he knew that their bond was even stronger now, both physically and emotionally. He kissed her forehead, and then, without thinking, leaned in to kiss her lips. Kiara, playfully pushing him away, giggled and darted toward the washroom. Sameer, grinning mischievously, scooped her up in his arms and carried her to the balcony, laughing all the way. There, in the soft light of morning, with the world waking up around them, they shared a moment of pure connection, feeling as though the day was theirs to create, full of love and promise. As they stood together on the balcony, the cool morning breeze tousled their hair, and the soft rays of sunlight painted a golden hue on their faces. The world outside seemed to stand still, as if acknowledging the intimacy of the moment they were sharing. Sameer wrapped his arms around her, holding her close as if to shield her from everything but the peacefulness of this shared space. "This is perfect," he whispered, his voice full of warmth. "Just you and me, no distractions, no worries."

"I've never felt more at peace," she replied softly. "I want the time to just stop. You know, I never thought I'd find someone like you. Someone who makes everything feel so special."

Sameer smiled, brushing a strand of hair away from her face. "I feel the same way," he said, his eyes locking with hers. "You've changed my world, Kiara. And I'm so grateful for that."

She leaned up and kissed him softly on the lips, a kiss full of love, promise, and an unspoken connection that had only deepened with time. The morning sun continued to rise, casting its golden light over them, and they knew that no matter what the future held, they had each other. Together, they felt ready to take on anything the world had to offer. He gently made her sit on the chair. It was as if he had plucked a fresh red rose and placed it delicately in a vase, careful not to wrinkle its delicate petals. With a quiet smile, he stepped away, heading inside to change into a crisp white linen shirt and boil some water for tea. She sat silently, her eyes following him from across the room, her thoughts wandering. He looks so strong and sturdy, yet he's so gentle with his touch. He's the perfect man. God doesn't make them like this anymore, she thought, a smile curling at the corner of her lips. As the steam from the boiling kettle fogged his spectacles, her gaze softened. He looked endearing with his shirt left unbuttoned at the collar, his beige shorts, and the round spectacles perched on his nose. It was the first time she had ever seen him wearing them, and for some reason, it made him seem even more appealing. Once, she would have scoffed at glasses, even despising the way they seemed to alter one's appearance. But with him, everything felt different. He returned to her holding a steaming cup of tea in his hands. She was still staring at him, lost in the warmth of the moment. As she took the cup from him and took a sip, the comforting warmth spread through her. "Earl Grey with a dash of lemon! It's my favourite, and it's perfectly made," she said, her voice soft with appreciation. "How do you know I like it?"

"Sweetheart, how can we be so close if I don't know these small details that make you happy?"

He leaned in, his lips pressing gently against hers in a soft, lingering kiss. It was a moment that seemed to stretch, as if time itself had paused to witness the tenderness of the gesture.

"I don't want to go back, but I should reach home today. My wife went to her hometown and will be back anytime tomorrow," he said, his voice heavy with a sense of reluctance.

Her smile faltered. She tried to hide the pain that suddenly welled up inside her, but the sting was impossible to ignore. She blinked rapidly; the warmth of the tea forgotten as her heart began to ache. He noticed the shift in her expression immediately. His eyes softened, and without thinking, he moved closer, taking her hands gently in his. The coolness of her skin contrasted with the heat of his touch. He wiped away a tear that had escaped from her eye, his thumb brushing against her cheek with a tenderness that made her breath catch in her throat.

"I should go and get ready."

"Baby, I want to join you," Sameer's voice, teasing and playful, echoed from a distance. Her laughter bubbled up instinctively, her eyes shining as she signalled him to hurry. The shower had always been a place of solace for her—a refuge where the steam and water could wash away not just the dirt, but the weight of the world. It was where she could cry freely, where the sound of the water could drown out the noise of her thoughts, letting her heart release whatever it needed. But today was different. Today, the shower was no longer a place for tears. Instead, it became a sacred space where two souls, exposed and vulnerable, met to celebrate their love. There were no barriers between them, no shields to hide behind. Today, love conquered the pain, and joy swept away the shadows of sadness. They stood together under the warmth of the water, not in solitude but in the beauty of their shared commitment. In that intimate moment, nothing else mattered—no past regrets, no unspoken fears. The only thing that felt real was their connection, their promise to each other. They were drenched, not just in water, but in love, faith, and a romance that felt as natural as the very air they breathed. The world outside had disappeared, leaving only them, two hearts bound in a moment of pure union, where nothing seemed more important than the love they shared. After the amazing moment they shared, Kiara and Sameer stepped out of the shower, their hearts still racing from the warmth of their connection. The air was thick with the remnants of their intimacy, but they both knew the day had to go on. With a sense of calm and contentment, they quickly got dressed and made their way to the restaurant, where the aroma of freshly brewed coffee and warm food filled the air. Breakfast was a simple affair, but it was perfect in its own way—a quiet, peaceful moment where the love they shared lingered, even in the smallest gestures. As they sat down to eat, the weight of the morning's emotions settled into a gentle sense of happiness. After a scrumptious breakfast, they planned to visit a couple of places - red fort, purana quilla, parathe wali gali, etc.

"I always had that indomitable wish to visit the historical Indian places described in our history textbooks," he said, his voice filled with nostalgia. "Alas, due to work pressure and the incessant traveling associated with it, I've had very few opportunities. I'm happy to have met you and even happier that I've come here with you. I never imagined I would get to visit this fort."

"Have you ever visited this place before?"

"First of all, I never had a boyfriend who was so enthusiastic about visiting historical places. And from the time I started working, I've been in Chennai. So, I'm grateful, too, that I'm finally visiting this marvel of architecture with a gem of a person like you!" Both laughed, the sound of their joy blending with the serenity of the surroundings.

Lost in conversation, time flew by. Sameer's stomach, however, had a way of reminding him that it had been hours since they'd eaten.

"I'm so hungry, Shona," he said, playfully rubbing his belly. "Can we go to a restaurant and have something appetizing?"

"We may not always find appetizing food inside concrete-walled, fancy places! Are you open to exploring?"

Confusion flickered across his face, but he managed to smile. "Can't quite understand what you mean, but I trust you."

Without waiting for any more explanations, she grabbed his hand and led him through the bustling streets of Old Delhi, to the famous "Paranthe Wali Gali" in Chandni Chowk. The tiny alley, full of life and rich with history, was a far cry from the polished restaurants he was accustomed to. The food at Paranthe Wali Gali was delectable, rich in flavour and tradition. Kiara had been here countless times, but this was her first time with him. She watched his face as he took in the chaotic charm of the place—dirt-streaked walls, narrow passageways, and sizzling hot paranthas being fried in open pots. Sameer, who was very conscious of class and always preferred more upscale places, seemed awestruck. He bit into a stuffed parantha, its crispness and warmth surprising him. "All that glitters and is expensive and cooked in olive oil isn't always tasty," he mused, his tone a mix of awe and realization.

Kiara smiled, amused by his reaction.

As they sat together, surrounded by the delicious smells and the hustle of the street, she couldn't help but feel a deep sense of satisfaction. After all, who would want to return to the glass and steel façades of office buildings, to coding or making PPTs, after an experience like this? But as all good things do, their time together was coming to an end.

He had to return to his family.

The ride to the airport was quiet. They both clung to each other's hands, the weight of the impending separation heavy between them. The tension was palpable, neither of them wanting to acknowledge the sadness looming over them. Their eyes were moist, and the silence in the car seemed endless. They exchanged no words, only occasional glances, both trying to savour every second together. At the airport, the weight of reality hit hard. He stood at the gate, unable to move, as if the very concrete of the airport was pulling him back. His emotions were so overpowering, he felt as though his feet were rooted to the ground. He couldn't tear his gaze away from her, the intensity of his grief making it feel impossible to take the next step.

"Promise me, baby," he said, his voice thick with emotion. "Promise me that whenever you happen to visit Mumbai, you will call me in advance."

Her eyes welled up. She opened her mouth to say yes, but the words got stuck in her throat.

"Won't you call me, Shona?" He asked, his voice soft but insistent.

Finally, after a long moment of hesitation, Kiara nodded, tears streaming down her face. She had promised, but it didn't stop the ache in her heart. Unable to hold it back any longer, she burst into tears, throwing herself into Sameer's arms. He held her tightly, his own tears threatening to fall as he comforted her. In that embrace, everything else faded away—time, space, and even the inevitable distance that would come between them. All that remained was the warmth of their love, the bond they had created, and the promise that it would endure, no matter the miles between them.

The time had come for both Kiara and Sameer, and it wasn't the harshness of a goodbye that lingered in their hearts, but the comforting words of "see you soon." It was those words they longed to hear, the promise of reuniting someday that softened the ache of separation. Their love had grown so deep over time, yet this time, Kiara couldn't bring herself to explain how wrong everything felt. She couldn't make him see that what they were doing was crossing a line, and they had unwittingly taken their love to a point where it could affect more lives than they realized. With wet cheeks and eyes that refused to dry, Kiara made her way through the airport taxi counter, walking away from him. He, too, stood at the same crossroads, his own heart heavy with the same unspoken words, until the moment passed, and they both turned away. She boarded the cab back to her PG, her thoughts swirling, while he was in the check-in queue at the airport, scrolling through emails on his phone. It was then that her name flashed across his screen which made him smile.

"What are you doing?" she asked, her voice a mix of curiosity and affection.

"Baby, I'm in the check-in queue," trying to mask the sadness in his voice. "The boarding pass printing machines seem to have a glitch."

"Don't you think something's off today? Are you sure you're not going to miss your flight and come back to me?"

Sameer's heart ached at the words. She wanted to demand that he stay, to make him realize how much she needed him, but instead, she settled for the quieter, more rational side of herself.

"I wish I could," he replied, laughing softly. "But I can't."

Even though she didn't want to be the understanding one, she sighed.

"Yeah, I understand… and I'll always understand."

The weight of her own words hit her harder than she expected. Sameer sensed it, felt the strain in her tone, and knew that if the conversation continued, it could end badly. He didn't want to sour the memory of their time together, so he made the decision to disconnect before it went further.

"Baby, my turn has come. Let me give you a call back once I settle down," he said gently, knowing she needed space.

"Okay, I'll take the taxi now back home."

Half an hour passed, and she was nearing her destination when her phone rang again. It was him.

"Where are you now?" he inquired, his voice full of the same concern that had never wavered between them.

"I'm about to reach home."

Sameer's voice softened, tinged with a sleepiness that matched her own. "I'm feeling so sleepy, but before I board the flight, I need a kiss, just so I can sleep peacefully."

"I'm in the cab, I can't do that."

"I need a kiss," he insisted, his voice warm, teasing, yet somehow serious.

She tried to distract him with other words, but his request lingered, impossible to ignore. She smiled despite herself, though it was fleeting, and by the time she had reached her PG, she was already stepping out of the cab, phone in hand. As she walked toward the entrance of her building, she pressed her lips to the phone screen, her kiss travelling across the distance. "I never thought I'd turn so digital when I fell in love," she murmured, half laughing, half crying.

He chuckled softly; his voice filled with quiet gratitude. "Thank you," he said. "You always know how to make me feel better."

"I don't know how long we'll be together, but today, I promise that I'll try to make every day of your life the best one."

They shared one last kiss over the phone before the call ended, leaving them both in the silence of their respective worlds, each carrying the weight of the same promise.

Kiara stayed in a non-sharing PG, which meant she had a tiny room, but the privacy it offered was priceless. After a long day, as she stood by the stove, stirring the bubbling pot of Maggie for dinner, she couldn't help but feel a sense of calm. It was one of those quiet moments that gave her a much-needed break from the hustle of life. While waiting for the noodles to cook, she picked up her phone and called Ananya. As the phone rang, Kiara smiled at the thought of their conversations—always long, filled with both silly anecdotes and deep reflections.

"Hey! How's it going?"

"I'm good! What's new with you?" Ananya replied, her voice warm and curious.

Kiara leaned back against the counter, her phone propped between her ear and shoulder. She began sharing the updates, recounting the little and big incidents that had filled her days. The tiny victories, the annoying setbacks, and the odd, quirky moments that somehow felt significant in their own way. She talked about the challenges of living alone, the satisfaction of independence, and the fleeting moments of loneliness that were still there despite the freedom. As the conversation continued, she felt grateful for these conversations, for Ananya's presence in her life, and for the privacy and peace her tiny room afforded her. By the time their conversation ended, her Maggie was ready. It was slightly soupy, just the way she liked it—comforting and warm, the perfect end to her busy day. She devoured it while humming along to some classic 70s Bollywood tunes, the familiar melodies filling the small room with nostalgia. With her dinner done, she leaned back against her bed, flipping through the latest issue of Gold-dust magazine, a mix of fashion tips and celebrity gossip that was her guilty pleasure.

As the hours passed in a hazy blur, Kiara lost track of time and drifted to sleep, the soothing combination of music, food, and the magazine making her feel relaxed and content. Before she knew it, the gentle hum of the phone's vibration pulled her from a deep, peaceful slumber. Groggy, she opened her eyes to see her phone screen lit up with notifications. There were twelve missed calls and a handful of messages from him. His latest message said, "Please don't return my call. I have reached home. I'll call you tomorrow when my wife is not around."

Kiara's heart sank for a moment, the reality of his situation hitting her like a cold wave. They could never be open, never truly connect in the way she wanted. But despite the complex emotions swirling in her chest, a small part of her felt a bittersweet happiness. He had tried to reach her, and that thought alone brought a smile to her face, even if only for a fleeting second. In a daze, she scrolled through her phone gallery. Her thumb moved almost instinctively as she flipped through picture after picture—over a hundred photos of the two of them, captured in moments of laughter, adventure, and closeness. Each photo held a memory, a snapshot of a time when they could pretend that the world didn't have its complications. They were just two people, sharing moments, living in the present, and for a while, that was enough. She stopped on a picture where they both were laughing, their faces illuminated by the warm glow of a sunset. It was one of her favorites, a reminder of the carefree days when everything seemed possible. She stared at the photo for a long while, her mind racing between reality and the small, tender moments they had shared. There was a sense of peace in the recognition that some things, no matter how complicated, were still worth cherishing. That entire night, she found herself lost in a whirlwind of thoughts and memories, visualizing every moment she and Sameer had shared.

Her mind replayed their time together over and over again. Only as dawn neared did exhaustion finally take over, and she was able to take a brief nap, her body and mind desperate for rest.

> "*The greatest pain that comes from love is loving someone you can't have.*"
>
> – *Unknown*

Gurgaon, 2011

Typing our Hearts Out

The alarm, however, was a rude awakening. The sharp, jarring sound sliced through the fog of her sleep-deprived state, instantly triggering a headache that only worsened as she forced herself out of bed. After rushing through her morning routine and popping a painkiller, she barely had time to catch her breath before heading out the door. Another day awaited her in the daily grind, and though the fatigue weighed heavily on her, there was a spark of excitement she couldn't shake off. She had a surprise in mind for Sameer, something special to brighten his day. At work, after catching up on emails and settling into the flow of the day, she took a moment to order a bouquet for him online. She composed an email, pouring her heart into it, apologizing for not taking his calls and expressing how much she missed him throughout the night.

Sameer, upon arriving at his workplace, opened his inbox and found her message. As he read it, a mix of emotions flooded him—he smiled and cried at the same time. His reply was a heartfelt response, an expression of his feelings for her:

> "You weren't exactly my love at first sight. But looking at you, I felt a radiant positive energy like a thousand suns, but as calm as the moon, as vast as the ocean, and as priceless as the 'Monalisa'; which simply wiped off my anger, frustration, and tiredness of the day. Your smile was like a drop of water in the middle of a desert. You were like the magic pill, which cured all diseases. Meeting you is a blessing."

Reading his words made her tear up.

"You might get another surprise today."

Sameer responded with a smiling emoticon, his excitement palpable.

Later that afternoon, he received the bouquet she had ordered. When he called her, his voice was full of warmth and gratitude. "Baby, what's this? I'm feeling so good and special. Everyone at work is asking if it's my birthday today."

She couldn't help but laugh. "Why don't you tell them you met the love of your life recently and made love in Delhi?"

Sameer burst out laughing too. "You really made my day," he said, still chuckling.

"I'm glad to hear that."

Their connection deepened, not just through calls, but especially through their email exchanges. Their inbox became a sanctuary for their thoughts, a space where they could pour out their hearts, share little details of their daily lives, and weave their emotions into words. It was as if each email was a letter from the soul, filled with dreams, longing, and laughter. They could talk about anything—from the mundane to the intimate—and every conversation felt like a treasure. Some might judge them, condemning their affair as a betrayal, as something that went against the rules of marriage. But to them, their love was something inexplicable, an emotional connection so deep that it transcended the barriers of convention. Love, they believed, wasn't something that could be controlled or rationalized. It just happened, sweeping them off their feet, offering a kind of euphoria that neither of them had ever experienced before. It was as if their souls had met across time and space, and nothing—no rules, no boundaries—could separate them. For them, love was an indescribable force, a warmth that wrapped around them, comforting them in a way nothing else ever had. Their connection was like two bodies with one heart, beating together in a rhythm that no one else could understand. The days turned into weeks, and then months. Their emails continued to flow back and forth, never missing a beat. Their love, despite the distance, grew stronger. Kiara began traveling for work more frequently, after successfully completing her first assignment in Chennai. Each new place she visited only made her miss Sameer more, but it also gave her the opportunity to share new experiences with him through their emails. No matter where they were in the world, no matter the time zone or the distance between them, a "Good morning" email from Kiara to Sameer was always a must, followed by his reply. It became their daily ritual, the one constant in their hectic lives, a simple yet powerful reminder that no matter what life threw at them, their love remained unshaken.

> "*They were a perfect couple; they were just not in the perfect situation.*"
>
> *– Unknown*

Gurgaon, 2011

In the Shadows of the Silence

One fine morning, as Sameer settled into his routine and checked his emails at work, he was surprised to see that there was no message from Kiara. He thought, perhaps, she was traveling, as she had hinted that she might need to go to Italy on short notice. He recalled a teasing conversation they'd had before she left.

He had jokingly said, "French women are most seducing, and so are Italian men. Who knows, you might end up with a hot boyfriend there!"

The remark had annoyed Kiara, but Sameer couldn't help but smile at the memory, shaking his head at his own teasing. "Why not I send her an email today and make her day?" he thought to himself. He quickly typed out a message:

> "I had a bad start this morning. There was no email from you. Where are you, my love? Write me back as soon as possible."

He hit send and waited, eager for her reply. But as the day stretched on, and then into the evening, no response came. By the next day, he found himself checking his inbox compulsively. Days passed, yet Kiara's inbox remained silent. His heart sank with each passing hour, and he grew increasingly worried when his calls to her went unanswered. Later, her number was switched off. For a whole week, his frustration grew, and he couldn't focus on anything—his work, his life—all consumed by thoughts of Kiara and her sudden disappearance. The anxiety gnawed at him, and he tried calling her again and again, praying to hear the usual ringtone rather than the dreaded "switched off" message. But his hopes were dashed each time, and his fear intensified. Due to security constraints at work, he couldn't check his official emails from his phone, so he spent hours in the office, arriving early and leaving late, hoping to catch a glimpse of an email from her. But nothing came. After nearly two weeks of this torment, he decided to send another email. This time, when sent the email, he received an out-of-office reply.

The automatic response stated: "Kiara is currently on illness leave due to a recent accident. For all work-related concerns, please reach out to her manager, Arjun. For personal matters, please contact 90********."

His heart dropped. Panic surged through him as he re-read the message several times. Without thinking clearly, he immediately dialled the number provided for personal concerns. His voice shook as he asked, "Hello, may I speak to Kiara?"

The response came from a calm, unfamiliar voice. "Hey, I'm Dr. Ananya, Kiara's cousin. She's currently in the

ICU, and her condition is critical. I'm sorry, but she won't be able to speak with you right now."

His mind went blank, the words reverberating in his head. His hands were trembling as he barely managed to say, "Okay," before quickly hanging up the phone. The shock was too overwhelming for him to process. The next day, he tried again, only to hear the same heartbreaking news from Ananya. She understood who he was but chose to stay silent about the details, maintaining a respectful distance. He couldn't bear it any longer. His heart was heavy with dread, and he felt helpless. On the third day, he received a call that would change everything. It was Ananya, but this time her tone was different—less clinical, more personal.

"Hi, I'm Dr. Ananya. Kiara is recovering from surgery, but her condition is still critical. I know you are Sameer—the one she met in Chennai and then in Delhi. Don't be surprised that I know all of this; Kiara has told me everything about you. She loves you, and I know that you love her too."

He felt a surge of emotions—relief, fear, and love all at once. But Ananya wasn't finished.

"Is it possible for you to come down here? Perhaps your presence, your love, can help her recover faster when our medicines cannot."

He was stunned, the words sinking into his mind like a heavy weight.

"Who's there with her?"

Ananya replied, her tone calm yet laced with sorrow, "Well, you do know that she doesn't have immediate parents. I'm here with my dad. My dad and I have been here for the past two weeks now. Dad cries and prays for her every day, hoping she'll open her eyes, but we haven't seen any signs of hope yet."

Sameer, trying to keep himself composed amidst the emotional turbulence, said, "How come you were so sure that it's me calling all these days?"

"Kiara is my younger self. She doesn't have many friends who would call again and again, asking about her well-being. The ones she has have already visited her. Will you come?" she asked again, her voice heavy with expectation.

He didn't reply.

Ananya's belief grew firmer with each passing second—that this man, whom Kiara loved so deeply, didn't love her the same way. She didn't ask again, knowing nothing would break through his silence.

Before hanging up, she said, "I'm texting the address to you."

"Okay," Ananya could feel the lump in his throat, the hesitation in his words.

"I know you're probably thinking, why am I taking so long to come, or why I am not saying yes. Things are complicated," he said, his voice shaking. "I'm not sure when I can come, but can you please tell me exactly what happened to her?"

Ananya's heart tightened at the sound of his broken voice. She sighed deeply before beginning to speak. "When all this happened, she was on the phone with me.

There was heavy blood loss, and she has a rare blood group, adding more complexity. I'm monitoring her continuously. The doctors are doing everything they can, but the chances of survival are bleak."

"As you know, she prefers taking the office cab. But that day, after she boarded the cab, the driver stopped at a roadside tea stall to grab something. While the driver was out, a lorry came at full speed and hit the car. The lorry was overloaded, and the driver lost control after a brake failure."

He was taken aback, trying to process the horrific image in his mind. He couldn't fathom it—his vibrant, fun-loving Kiara, now fighting for her life in a hospital bed, uncertain if she would even survive, and if she did, whether she would ever be the same again. The idea that she might live as a shell of the person she once was, or worse, never regain control of her body, was unbearable.

"Are you there?"

He struggled to hold back the sobs threatening to escape. His thoughts raced, and the reality of the situation seemed too overwhelming to grasp. Finally, he managed to ask, his voice barely a whisper, "Can you promise me… you'll take good care of her?"

Ananya heard him sobbing over the call, her heart heavy with sympathy for both. "I will. Take care of yourself, Sameer. Let me know whenever you plan to visit her."

He hung up, his heart weighed down with guilt, regret, and an overwhelming sense of helplessness. That night, he returned home with a heavy heart, lost in thought.

His mind spiralled as he wondered if his actions had led to this crossroads—his family on one side, and his love for Kiara on the other. The urge to be there for her was strong, and part of him wanted to book a flight to Delhi the next morning. But memories of the last time he went to see Kiara stopped him. On that trip, when he returned from Delhi, his wife had discovered the flight booking details. She had checked the fine print and uncovered the truth—he hadn't gone on an official trip, but rather a personal one to meet Kiara. The confrontation had been ugly, and it had almost led to a divorce. Only after pleading with her, citing the kids and promising never to do something like this again, did his wife give him one last warning. She told him that if she found out he was talking to Kiara or trying to meet her again, she would leave him and take the kids with her. Now, with his wife's suspicions at an all-time high, he knew he couldn't risk another confrontation. She had become more vigilant, tracking everything he did, almost as though there was a spy following him everywhere.

He was trapped.

He stood under the hot water of the shower, tears mingling with the water as he sobbed in silence. His mind was consumed by the thought of Kiara. The weight of his situation, his heart torn between his family and his love for Kiara, was unbearable. Kiara's words echoed in his mind: "The day you realize this relationship isn't going anywhere, we'll both be hurt deeply; some damages are irreparable."

It hit him like a thunderbolt. The truth of her words stung—he should have ended things with her earlier. The damage had already been done. There was no way back.

Days passed, and Sameer's calls to Ananya dwindled, while Ananya's calls to him increased. Every day, she called to check when he would come to visit Kiara, her hopes slowly fading as the days went on. Sameer never directly answered her questions. Instead, he continued to ask for updates about Kiara, insisting on receiving pictures. After some hesitation, Ananya finally agreed and sent him a few photos.

When he saw the pictures, his heart broke. Kiara, once full of life, was now a shadow of herself. Her body was covered in bandages and bruises. Machines surrounded her, with multiple tubes and wires connected to various parts of her body, needles piercing her skin. A tube was inserted into her nose, and another down her throat. Sameer's heart ached with guilt and helplessness. He wanted nothing more than to hold her, to feel her heartbeat, to rest her head on his chest, to caress her hair, and to look deep into her eyes. He wanted to love her more than ever before, but he was powerless. After almost six weeks, she began to show signs of life. She could make faint noises, like a baby learning to speak. She signalled for Ananya to give her the phone and asked her to call Sameer. Ananya dialled his number, warning him not to tell Kiara that he had never visited her or that he planned to visit soon. He agreed, saying, "Don't worry. she understands me. She'll understand this time too."

When the phone was put on speaker, he could hear Kiara's shallow breaths. He spoke softly, trying to hide the pain in his voice. "Hi baby, please don't try to speak. Let me talk. I missed you so much. I missed your e-mails, but you know what? Today is my 'bonus' day."

Kiara was confused, struggling to comprehend his words. "What?"

"You know why? Because we are talking today. I can picture your face. It calms me down, baby. You don't have to worry about anything. You just need to rest and get better. We'll meet soon. For now, take it easy, okay? I'm not there physically, but I'll be there soon. I love you."

He could hear her trying to speak, her voice faint and laboured. He blew a kiss into the phone, then the call was taken from her by Ananya, who stepped outside.

Ananya's voice was filled with anger as she confronted him. "Please don't give her false hope when she's slowly dying! You're just torturing her with these lies."

"I'm trying to figure out how to come. I have to be careful this time, because if my wife finds out… my life will be destroyed."

"Your life should be destroyed because you've destroyed one here. She may not be mature enough to understand, but you are. You have a wife and kids, yet you've been living this double life, not realizing the damage you've caused. Why didn't you stop her? Why didn't you stop yourself from this mess? She always understood you, always found a way to talk to you, to keep you happy, but now, God damn it, she needs you."

He remained silent, unable to respond. The tension hung heavily in the air. Ananya's emotions finally boiled over, and she snapped, "You are a spineless creature! You've been using her for your own physical satisfaction. It was never love for you. You won't be forgiven, not ever. Karma is a bitch, and you'll get what you deserve. If you ever call her again, I swear, I'll file an FIR against you, or even better, I'll call your wife and tell her everything."

With that, Ananya disconnected the call. For the first time in weeks, she felt a strange sense of relief, as if a heavy burden had been lifted from her chest. She no longer felt the need to hold back, no longer afraid of confronting Sameer. The truth had to come out, and she had no intention of staying silent any longer.

Meanwhile, Arjun, Kiara's manager, visited her every day at the hospital. Ananya couldn't help but admire Arjun's genuine care for Kiara. She could see that he wasn't faking it; his concern for her was real. As days passed, Arjun and Ananya became inseparable in their efforts to keep Kiara's spirits up. Arjun would tell her stories, make her laugh, and talk about the small details from work to distract her from the pain. Ananya noticed the subtle shift in their bond, with Arjun slowly falling for Kiara, though Kiara's heart still seemed to belong to Sameer. Her eyes kept on asking Ananya about Sameer.

One fine day when she again asked about Sameer, Ananya couldn't take it any longer. She said, "I feel that he had only been interested in the physical aspects of relationship you have with him. I don't think he cares about you. I have made numerous calls to him, begging him to come, all of which had been ignored. Please stop thinking about him. From past few days, he hasn't even called and ask whether you are alive or dead."

To make her believe, Ananya showed her the call records and numerous messages she has sent to Sameer.

Kiara's face, once filled with sadness and confusion, immediately transformed. The hurt and heartbreak seemed to dissipate, replaced by a sense of clarity and resolve. For a moment, she became someone unrecognizable—the confident, assertive woman she had always been before Sameer's intrusion in her life.

"If you are not lying then I've been a fool all this while," Kiara said, her voice steady. "I tried to fool myself into believing that he cared. Everyone who knew about my relationship with him tried to show me the truth, but I didn't want to see it. It's over, Ananya. It's over."

Kiara appeared no longer the broken, lost girl who had been clinging to a toxic relationship. "I'm tired of crying, of worrying about someone who doesn't care, of reaching out to someone who can't be mine. I almost destroyed a happy marriage in the process, and now I feel guilty. I'm done with this facade of smiling while I'm breaking inside."

There were no tears in her eyes anymore. Whether it was because she had truly found the strength to let go, or if she was simply pretending to be strong, Ananya couldn't tell. However, Kiara's transformation was clear. She had made a choice, a painful but necessary one.

Arjun reached for Kiara's hand, squeezing it gently.

"You must move on, Kiara. We must move on," he said softly.

"It's not easy decision but sometime walking away is the best thing you could do for yourself and for everyone around you who loves you deeply, trusting that there is something better waiting for you," said Arjun.

"You're right, Arjun," said Ananya.

> "*People come into your life for a reason, season, or a lifetime*"
>
> – *Brian A. Chalker.*

You loved Sameer thinking that he will be there with you for a lifetime but that's not the case, darling.

Kiara nodded faintly, the ghost of a smile crossing her lips. Her eyes weren't filled with hope, but there was a quiet sense of peace. Whether this was the beginning of true healing or just a temporary reprieve, only time would tell. But for now, she was ready to step forward.

Few days later, when Sameer was about to leave his workplace, he received a message from Ananya. It left him speechless and devastated.

"Kiara passed away. Please do not call."

Despite her explicit warning not to call, he couldn't control his emotions and dialled her number.

Ananya was sobbing on the call. Sameer, broken, was unable to hold back his grief, feeling overwhelmed by the loss of the woman he loved.

"I can never see her again! I so wish I could have visited her," he cried, the weight of his regret and sorrow crushing him.

Ananya, though hurt and angry at him, could sense his pain. After a few moments, he gathered himself and asked, "When did it happen?"

"Almost an hour ago," Ananya replied quietly.

"Did she leave any message for me?"

"No. She loved you and will always love you. But now, you don't need to worry about how you'll manage with your wife and kids on one side, and her on the other. Do you realize she made it so easy for you? She kept her promise of helping you find happiness and peace, even while going through her own suffering."

Ananya paused, the anger and sadness mixing in her voice before she added, "Please, don't spoil anyone else's life now," and ended the call.

Sameer was left alone with his guilt, his grief, and his shattered heart. He understood, perhaps for the first time, the full extent of the damage he had done—both to Kiara and to his own life.

Do you think their love would have been complete if Kiara was alive?

Their love, in its purest form, was one of deep connection and passion, but it was also tangled in the complexity of Sameer's commitments and Kiara's sacrifices. If Kiara had survived, the path ahead for them would have been fraught with difficult choices, guilt, and the ongoing struggle between love and responsibility. It's hard to say if they could have truly completed their love, given the circumstances—Sameer's obligations to his family and the tension that Kiara's presence created in his life. Perhaps their love would have always been incomplete in a worldly sense, yet in their hearts, it was unbreakable.

Love stories are often bound by time and circumstances. Sometimes, the most intense love stories are those that remain unfinished, left in the realm of what could have been. Kiara and Sameer's love was like that—intense, but tragically cut short, leaving behind an unspoken promise of what could have been.

> "*Sometimes, we love people we can never have, and the pain of that unfinished love lives with us, like a shadow that never fades.*"
>
> – *Unknown*

10 Years Later

Her fingers trembled as she picked up the phone in the middle of the night from an unfamiliar number flashing on the screen. Placing the conch back on the mantlepiece, her heart raced as she held the phone to her ear, trying to process the voice on the other end. Her mind quickly went through the possibilities, but none made sense. The voice, thick with emotion, was unmistakable, and yet so out of place. "I miss you; I really do! Something inside me kept on telling me all these years that you are still around, and I wasn't surprised when I saw your image on the cover of your book at crosswords. Why did you lied to me," the voice cracked with emotion, and Kiara's heart clenched in her chest. Her mind shot back to the past, to a time she'd buried deep, one that she'd almost forgotten.

Kiara closed her eyes, the weight of those words sinking in, and the years of silence between them seemed to vanish in an instant. It was like no time had passed at all. She could feel the intensity in his voice, the pain of unspoken words, the loss they had both suffered. She had buried that pain deep within her, but now, it was resurfacing with an intensity she hadn't expected.

"How did you get my number?" she managed to ask, her voice trembling.

"That doesn't matter. Tell me, do you miss me?"

She felt her pulse quicken as he continued, the weight of his words pressing heavily on her. "Kiara," he whispered, his voice barely a breath. "I've tried to forget you. I've tried to move on… but it's like I can't breathe without you."

A lump formed in her throat, and she fought to keep her composure. She had moved on, or so she had told herself. She was married, with a life that seemed perfect on the surface. But beneath it all, the memories of her time with him—the passion, the connection—had never truly faded. How could they?

"I don't understand why you're calling me now," she replied, her voice unsteady. "I've moved on."

But deep down, she knew the truth. She hadn't really moved on. Not from him. Not from what they had shared. The love they once had, the love that had never been given a chance to flourish, still lingered in the depths of her heart. The line went silent for a long moment, and she could hear him breathing, trying to steady himself. Then, he spoke again, his words raw with emotion. "I just needed to hear your voice one more time. I needed to know if you still… if you ever missed me."

Kiara's eyes closed as the weight of those words hit her. The past flooded her mind—the laughter, the moments they had shared, the love they had once believed could overcome all obstacles. She had tried to bury those feelings, tried to forget, but they were always there, just beneath the surface.

"Some are destined to find and cherish love, while others, like us, just get a glimpse of it and are left with nothing but the memories," she murmured, her voice trembling as she repeated the words he had once written to her.

The line went quiet once again. This time, there would be no more words. No more explanations. She didn't need to say anything else. The past was the past, but the scars it had left on both would last forever. The love they had shared would remain as a memory—one that would never fully fade, no matter how hard they tried.

Kiara set the phone down, the tears that she had held back for so long threatening to spill over. It was over. It had always been over.

This is Kiara signing off.

www.ingramcontent.com/pod-product-compliance
Lightning Source LLC
LaVergne TN
LVHW091301150826
845673LV00006B/1500

* 9 7 9 8 8 9 6 7 3 8 1 5 2 *